"My relationship with James,"

Amanda said coolly, "is none of your business. I don't want to discuss it with you."

"I think it is. I think I have a right to know. After all, you did break our engagement for him." Drew's face was etched with stern lines.

"You have no rights," she breathed in protest, suddenly angry. "Tell me, Drew, while we were engaged, were all your business trips as cozy as this?"

Amanda indicated the intimate table, the romantic restaurant, with an expressive sweep of one delicate hand. "Or is this reserved for business associates who are a little more stubborn when it comes to falling into bed with you?"

KATHRYN ROSS was born in Zambia, where her parents happened to live at the time, but was educated in Ireland and England. She now lives in a village near Blackpool in Lancashire. She enjoys her work as a professional beauty therapist, but the main love of her life is writing. Kathryn doesn't remember a time when she wasn't scribbling— her first novel at the age of ten was a children's adventure story, unpublished but terrific! Traveling and the friends made through it has been a real pleasure. Candlelit dinners, log fires on a winter's night and long walks in the Lake District are also special joys. She says she's naturally romantic, enjoying reading as well as writing romantic fiction. Mr. Right hasn't come along yet, though, Kathryn admits her boyfriends have tough competition from her fictional heroes.

KATHRYN ROSS

designed with love

Harlequin Books

TORONTO • NEW YORK • LONDON
AMSTERDAM • PARIS • SYDNEY • HAMBURG
STOCKHOLM • ATHENS • TOKYO • MILAN

Harlequin Presents first edition August 1990
ISBN 0-373-11294-7

Original hardcover edition published in 1989
by Mills & Boon Limited

Copyright © 1989 by Kathryn Ross. All rights reserved.
Except for use in any review, the reproduction or utilization
of this work in whole or in part in any form by any electronic,
mechanical or other means, now known or hereafter invented,
including xerography, photocopying and recording,
or in any information storage or retrieval system, is forbidden without
the permission of the publisher, Harlequin Enterprises Limited,
225 Duncan Mill Road, Don Mills, Ontario, Canada M3B 3K9.

All the characters in this book have no existence outside the
imagination of the author and have no relation whatsoever to
anyone bearing the same name or names. They are not even
distantly inspired by any individual known or unknown to the
author, and all incidents are pure invention.

® are Trademarks registered in the United States Patent and
Trademark Office and in other countries.

Printed in U.S.A.

CHAPTER ONE

THERE was an attractive exuberance about Amanda as she hurried out of the taxi and up the steps to her father's office block. She felt good being back in London, and, most importantly, back at work. Three weeks was just too long to be away.

The doorman tipped his hat and smiled admiringly at her. His eyes appraised her willowy model-girl figure and the golden, flame-coloured hair that cascaded over her shoulders in luxuriant waves.

'Good morning, Miss Hunter.' He swung open the heavy glass doors with their gold-embossed emblem of Hunter Fashions.

'Thank you, John.' Her voice was low and well modulated, with husky undertones that had a disturbing effect on the male pulse-rate. That she was oblivious to this fact only seemed to add to her fascination.

She crossed the white marble floor towards the lifts, and for a moment when the doors opened she had a clear view of herself in their mirrored interior. The soft turquoise-blue suit that she was wearing looked superb with her dramatic colouring, her skin radiant and flawless. Her eyes, thickly fringed with dark lashes, were a deep emerald shade, but today they shimmered with blue lights, reflecting the turquoise of her outfit. Three weeks spent in the cool mountain air of the Swiss Alps had added to her a glow of radiant beauty.

She stepped inside the lift and turned her back on her reflection. She wasn't interested in her looks; her one overriding preoccupation in life was her work.

She loved the creativity of designing beautiful clothes, outfits that would transform a woman and give her joy whenever she looked into a mirror. Yet she herself got no real pleasure out of wearing them; she had no wish to look desirable. She was a true career girl, as she often told her father when he hinted that, at twenty-six, she should be thinking of marriage.

Men and marriage were definitely at the bottom of Amanda's list of priorities. Only once had she made the mistake of thinking herself in love with someone. It was an episode that had taught her a bitter lesson. Now she guarded her body and her heart with a cool determination.

The lift came to a halt on the top floor, and she hurried down the corridor straight to the outer office. She hoped her father would have time to talk with her, for she had some very exciting ideas about next season's designs which she couldn't wait to tell him about.

'Hello, Sandy.' She smiled with friendly good humour at her father's private secretary. 'Any chance of my having a few words with the boss?'

The young girl looked up in surprise and covered the mouthpiece of the phone she had been speaking into. 'Miss Hunter! I didn't think you were due back until tomorrow.'

'No, I'm not, but I just can't keep away from the place.' Amanda moved towards the inner office door. 'Is it all right if I go in, or has he someone with him?'

'Wait a moment, Miss Hunter.' There was a note of gravity in the girl's voice which told Amanda instantly that all was not well. 'I'm afraid your father hasn't come in yet.'

She looked at the girl incredulously. 'He's not ill, is he?' Fear clutched at her heart. As far back as she could remember, her father had never missed a day at the office and he was never late. In a lot of ways the two of them were very alike: they both thrived on hard work and devoted themselves entirely to the Hunter Fashions emporium.

'I don't know.' Sandy's eyes clouded with worry. 'I don't know where he is, I've been trying to locate him all morning.'

'What about Saunders, did he have an idea where he could be?' Saunders was her father's major domo, a reliable man who made sure that everything in Donald Hunter's house ran with smooth efficiency.

'No, he said Mr Hunter left for work as usual at seven-thirty.' Sandy frowned. 'I can't understand it, it's just not like him. He has a very important meeting at ten-thirty. I went ahead and showed the client into your father's office; I felt sure he would arrive in time for it.'

'How long has he been waiting?' Amanda asked anxiously.

'Nearly twenty minutes, and I don't think he's accustomed to waiting around for anyone.'

'Who is he? Anyone I know?'

Before Sandy could answer she was sidetracked by the person she had been speaking to on the phone returning on the line. 'He's not there? Well, thank you for looking. If he does come in, will you ask him to ring his office?' She put the receiver down and looked at Amanda. 'Well, he's not at his club.'

Amanda's eyebrows rose. 'You surely don't think he would be there at this time of day?'

'I don't know what to think. Your father has been very on edge lately.' Sandy dropped her voice to a low whisper. 'I think it has something to do with the man waiting in his office. He's been in and out of here a lot over the last few weeks.'

Amanda looked thoughtfully towards the connecting office door. 'I'll go in and speak with him.'

'Oh, would you?' Sandy sounded relieved. 'I hope he's not too angry at being kept waiting. I think he must be someone very important, because your father has been treating him very confidentially.'

Amanda frowned. That didn't sound like her father at all. 'He's probably some awkward prospective customer. I'll soon deal with him.' She moved towards the door. 'You continue to ring around to find Dad.'

Amanda was extremely proficient at dealing with any business matter concerning Hunter Fashions. Being one of the top designers, she knew the business in depth and she often stood in for her father on sales trips and meetings. *She* had no doubt that it wouldn't take her long to placate the man, and probably get a large order from him as well.

Her father's office was dark compared with the fluorescent lighting of the other room. She moved further in, a calm, composed smile firmly in place.

'I'm very sorry to keep you waiting, Mr——' Her voice wavered precariously as her eyes came to rest on the broad-shouldered frame of the man who was standing with his back to her at the window. Dear God, she thought wildly, it couldn't be! It just couldn't be him.

He turned slowly to face her. 'Surely you haven't forgotten me, Amanda? Not after all we meant to each other.' His voice was amused, its deep, attractive timbre making her shiver inside. She hadn't heard that voice for over a year now, but she had never forgotten it, or the man who was staring at her now with deeply penetrating dark eyes.

Amanda's breath caught in her throat; she couldn't move, she couldn't speak. For a moment she wondered if she was seeing things. Drew Sheldon was the last man on earth she had expected—or wanted—to see.

'Don't tell me you're lost for words!' Drew looked at her stunned face with a derisive smile. 'What happened to the profuse apologies and the winning smile?' The question broke the spell that held her transfixed.

'What the hell are you doing here?' Her voice sounded dry and husky, and she swallowed on the blockage in her throat.

'Ah, that's more like the Amanda I used to know, as sweet and good-natured as ever,' he drawled sarcastically. He stretched out one lean hand and flicked on the overhead light. 'And twice as sexy,' he murmured.

Bright golden light brought everything into sharp focus. She could feel the hot colour flooding her face as his dark eyes locked with hers and then moved downwards, subjecting her body to a leisurely perusal. She wanted to turn away from him, but her body didn't seem to want to move and her eyes refused to be dragged away.

She had spent a long time trying to get the image of those strong features scrubbed from her memory, and as she looked at him now she knew she had never really succeeded. Every contour of his tanned, olive-toned skin was achingly familiar. He had a hard-boned, arrogantly attractive face, and her eyes lingered on the ruggedly jutting chin and the curve of his sensual mouth which had once kissed her so passionately.

'How have you been?' His deep voice broke the silence, urbane and polite.

She almost felt like laughing hysterically. The last time she had seen Drew they had quarrelled viciously and she had practically thrown her engagement ring back at him. Now he was politely enquiring after her health.

'Just exactly what do you want?' Her voice wasn't as steady as she would have liked.

His eyebrows rose. 'Are you always so rude to your father's business associates?'

'Only the ones we can do without.' She frowned. 'Anyway, since when have you become a business associate? You own hotels, not fashion boutiques.'

'Let's just say I like to keep my interests wide and varied.' He leaned indolently back against the window-frame. 'Where is your father, anyway?'

'I have no idea,' she answered crisply. 'Obviously he didn't think his appointment with you was worth keeping.'

Drew didn't look perturbed by her statement; instead he was watching her with amusement. She could feel anger and resentment boiling up inside her like a volcano ready to erupt. God, how she hated him; he was the most infuriating, galling man! The sensations teeming inside her were very familiar where he was concerned. He had always had the ability to arouse her emotions to fever-pitch. She had loved him, then hated him, and both feelings had been more intense than any other in her life.

'Somehow I get the impression that you're not very pleased to see me,' he said drily.

'My goodness, you *are* quick on the uptake!' She matched his sarcasm with a lightness of tone she was proud of. 'Now, if you would like to leave, I have a lot of work to attend to.'

He completely disregarded her request. 'You're not due back to work until tomorrow. Couldn't you find anything more exciting to do with your last day's holiday?'

'I'll come into the office any time it damn well pleases me, and it's none of your business how I choose to spend my time.' She glared at him, feeling the composure she had been trying so desperately to cling on to desert her completely. 'How did you know I was on holiday, anyway?'

'Your father mentioned it.' He was watching her with a glinting little smile that was profoundly disturbing. Even more unsettling was the news that her father had been discussing her with him. Before she could contemplate the implications of that, the intercom on her father's desk interrupted the heavy silence.

'There's a Ms Lee on line one for Mr Sheldon,' Sandy announced clearly.

Drew straightened and walked towards the phone. There was something dangerous and powerful about the way he moved. Beneath the exquisitely cut dark suit his body was hard-muscled, with broad shoulders and narrow hips. His strong, commanding presence seemed to dominate the large office, making Amanda feel small and insignificant, almost as if she were the interloper.

'Hello, Jordan.' He settled himself easily into her father's leather chair behind the desk. Amanda could feel a wave of hot fury burn her face at the sheer audacity of the man. How dared he sit there?

'Yes, I've been delayed,' Drew was saying smoothly. 'I probably won't be able to make our meeting until lunch time.' His eyes watched Amanda as he spoke and there was an insolent smile in them as he noted the angry heightened colour of her face.

'How are those figures looking?' he enquired lazily of the woman on the other end of the line, and then gave a low rumble of laughter at whatever had been the reply. The sound made Amanda's heart miss a beat, and she clenched her hands into tight fists at her sides until the knuckles gleamed white.

'Stop worrying, Jordan. Have you ever known a deal not to swing in my favour?' He was still smiling as he replaced the receiver. 'That was my accountant. I had an appointment with her at twelve.' He glanced at his watch and then back up at Amanda, taking in the tenseness of her stance with a narrowed-eyed look.

'Why don't you sit down and relax? You look very uptight.'

Her eyes flashed fire at him, their green suddenly brilliant in the smooth oval of her face. 'You're sitting in my father's chair.' Resentment made her words sound stiff and petty, and the minute she had said them she regretted them.

A gleam of masculine amusement lit his face. 'Your father isn't here.'

'No, and when he's not here, that is where *I* sit.' Amanda met his eyes defiantly; she was damned if she was going to sit at the wrong side of the desk in her own father's office.

A smile curved Drew's lips and she got the distinct impression that he was restraining himself from laughing at her with great difficulty. The feeling made her blood boil; it also gave her an uneasy sensation in the pit of her stomach that Drew Sheldon knew something that she didn't.

He scraped the chair back from the desk and for one surprised moment she thought he was going to vacate the chair for her. The thought was short-lived.

'If you're so anxious to sit this side of the desk, perhaps we can compromise and share the seat.' He patted his lap and looked at her with a humorous light in his dark eyes.

'You know, Drew, I'm really surprised by the fact that you have a female accountant, because you're still a chauvinistic brute.' Her voice trembled with fury.

'And you, my darling Amanda, are as bad-tempered, petulant and immature as you ever were.' He said the words softly, but they still stung her like physical blows. 'You take yourself far too seriously; whatever happened to that delightful sense of humour of yours?'

'Just get out of here, Drew.' Her eyes were cold, her voice bleak. She could have told him what had happened to that sense of fun she used to have. It had died along with all the other unprofitable feelings that had once accompanied it. Died along with the realisation that only a fool fell in love with a man like Drew Sheldon, and she was no longer a naïve fool. 'You're not welcome here, and you never will be.'

'Is that so?' he murmured, the gleam of amusement back on his face. 'We'll have to see about that.'

Amanda shivered. She didn't like that look; for some strange reason it frightened her.

The door opened behind her and she swung around, relief flooding through her at the sight of her father.

'Dad, where on earth have you been? We've been so worried!' Her relief turned to concern as she noted how tired her father looked. There was a grey, pallid tinge to his skin and a worried light in his blue eyes as they rested on her.

'Amanda, I didn't expect you back until tomorrow! How was Switzerland?' He came over and embraced her warmly.

'Beautiful.' As she pulled away from him she noticed he wasn't listening. His eyes were on Drew and there was a strange expression in them. Almost as if he were asking some silent question. 'I'm sorry to keep you waiting so long, Drew.'

'Don't worry about it, your daughter and I have been having a pleasant little chat about old times,' replied Drew easily.

'That's good.' Her father seemed to relax visibly.

Amanda looked disparagingly over at Drew as he came forward to shake her father's hand. Pleasant little chat, indeed! Who did he think he was kidding? She was about to say something to the contrary when Drew looked straight at her. There was no amusement now in those dark eyes, they seemed to pierce straight through her with a direct warning: keep quiet or else.

Amanda remained silent, her nerves quivering from the impact of those eyes. It had almost been like a small electric shock. No wonder the man was so successful in business; behind that charming, relaxed façade there was a ruthless, forceful man who would allow no one to cross him. What was he doing here? A chill shiver of fear ran through her. Surely her father wasn't doing any business with him? She watched the two men thoughtfully.

Donald Hunter was a tall, handsome man, ruggedly built, with only a sprinkling of grey in his dark hair, yet next to Drew he looked frail and old. As successful as her father was, he would be no match for the dynamic thirty-five-year-old businessman. Drew would devour him for breakfast. Just what the hell was Drew playing at? she wondered feverishly.

'How's your mother, Amanda?' her father asked now.

'Fine.' She didn't expand on her answer, which was unusual for Amanda. Usually when either of her parents enquired after the other she would launch into de-

scriptive detail. They had been divorced for years, yet
Amanda always held on to the hope that they would get
back together. Today she was too preoccupied with her
worried thoughts. 'Just what's been going on here while
I've been away?' She frowned at the ashen look on her
father's face. Was he being intimidated by Drew in some
way? 'Why are you so late coming in this morning?'

'I had an appointment which took longer than I
expected,' her father answered heavily. He walked over
towards the drinks cabinet and picked up a gleaming
cut-glass decanter. 'Let's all have a drink, then we can
sit and discuss things.'

'Perhaps coffee would be better,' Drew suggested
gently.

Donald's hand hovered over the glasses before he
turned around. 'Yes, you're right. I'll ask Sandy to make
us some.' He moved and opened the connecting office
door.

While her father spoke to his secretary, Drew moved
closer towards her. 'Just be very careful, Amanda,' he
warned in a softly menacing tone. 'Any juvenile displays
of your temper and you'll have me to deal with.'

'And just what is that supposed to mean?' She glared
at him with a bravado she was far from feeling.

'It means, behave like a mature woman, not an
emotional adolescent—or else...' His voice trailed off
as her father came back to join them. The implied threat
hung heavily over her, like an axe that was about to fall.

'It's nice to see you two getting on so well together
again,' Donald said, noticing their closeness and mis-
construing it.

'Yes, almost like old times, isn't it?' Drew placed a
light arm around Amanda's shoulders. The warmth of
his touch sent shudders through her body. She made to
pull away from him, but his grip tightened painfully on
the top of her arm, forcing her to stand still.

'I'm glad, it makes things so much easier.' Her father moved towards the soft easy chairs beside the drinks cabinet and sat down with a heavy sigh.

Easier for whom? Amanda wondered, a cold feeling of dread spiralling up inside.

Sandy tapped on the door and entered the room with a tray of coffee which she placed on the table at the side of Donald Hunter. Amanda noticed the way the girl smiled over at Drew as she quietly left them again. It was a look she was horribly familiar with. Drew held a fascination for women. His hard, lean good looks and the lazy, amused smile in his dark eyes captivated them. He could turn the most mature woman into a blushing, bemused girl with just the rise of a calculated eyebrow.

'Well, are you going to tell me what this is all about?' Amanda wrenched herself away from Drew and moved to glare impatiently at her father. He seemed to blanch even whiter under her green, intense scrutiny.

'I've sold Hunter Fashions.' The words were said in such a dull, flat tone that for a moment Amanda thought she hadn't heard correctly.

'You've what?' She expelled her breath in a startled gasp.

'I signed the contracts two weeks ago. Everything's sold. Lock, stock and barrel, as they say.' Her father's lips twisted in a humorous smile, but his eyes were serious as he watched his daughter's distress. 'Nobody knows yet; I've waited for you to come back so that I could tell you first.'

Amanda shook her head, she still couldn't believe what she was hearing. 'But why? Why, Dad?'

'Because it was time—time I started to relax and enjoy my life.'

'I don't believe you.' Amanda's voice trembled. Her father loved the business, it was his life just as it was hers. She swung around, her eyes narrowed accusingly on Drew. 'This is your doing, isn't it? You've somehow got a hold over my father and forced him to sell his business.' Her voice was filled with loathing and rage. 'I'll never forgive you for this, Drew, never!'

'I don't need your forgiveness, Amanda.' He lounged back against the desk. Only the hard glitter in his eyes belied his relaxed attitude. 'I made your father a very fair offer for the business and he accepted it.'

'You can't be serious!' All the burning colour drained from her face, leaving her delicate skin almost translucent. 'Father, you can't sell Hunter Fashions to this—this viper!' Her voice held an unconscious note of pleading.

'Too late, the viper already has possession.' There was a hint of menace in Drew's soft reply.

'You're just being ridiculous, Amanda,' her father put in. 'Drew made me an over-generous offer; he's taken all the pressure off me and handled everything with a speed and efficiency you just wouldn't believe.'

'Oh, yes, I would.' Amanda's voice shook. 'I'm sure Drew is very competent at rushing a sale when it's to his advantage. You don't for one moment think he's doing anything out of the kindness of his heart, do you?' Her voice was heavy with sarcasm. 'I've got news for you, Father: Drew Sheldon will destroy everything you've worked so hard to build—everything.'

Donald Hunter's face was ashen as he listened to his daughter, but Amanda's anger was so all-consuming that she didn't even notice. 'Have you stopped to wonder why a multi-millionaire with hotels scattered around the world would be interested in a small fashion house and a few boutiques?' she demanded harshly.

'That is enough.' Drew's controlled voice was as cold and cutting as ice. It held Amanda's tirade sharply in check. 'Whatever you might say, the fact remains that I am now in control of the business. Any ideas you wish to deliver on the subject, you can do so to me at nine o'clock tomorrow morning.'

Amanda stared at him blankly. 'I'll never set foot in these offices again.'

'Don't be silly, darling,' her father said soothingly. 'And there's no reason for you to worry about your job, it's quite secure.'

'Secure?' Amanda's eyes were wide and incredulous.

'That's right.' Donald Hunter gave his first real smile of the day. 'Nobody will lose their jobs. I think everyone will be happy with the arrangement. In fact, I've arranged a party at the house so that people can meet their new boss informally, and it will be a lovely celebration for us all.'

'Well, I won't be celebrating.' Amanda's voice was acid-dry. 'I'd rather die than work for Drew Sheldon.' She turned and moved stiffly towards the door, upsetting the table as she passed it, spilling cold coffee over its polished surface.

'Amanda!' Her father's voice called out after her, but she closed the door firmly and resolutely behind her.

'Anything wrong, Miss Hunter?' Sandy looked up, stunned by the furious expression on Amanda's face.

'Yes, everything.' Amanda headed out of the building as fast as she could. Everything was more than wrong, she thought bleakly. In one short morning her well-ordered world had been turned upside down, and it was all that vile, scheming man's fault. Why had he come back into her life again? God knew, he had created enough havoc the last time.

It was a relief to be out in the cold air, to feel the rain against her burning skin. She walked unheeding of the weather, her mind racing in circles. Of course, the reason why Drew Sheldon had come back was blindingly obvious—he wanted revenge.

CHAPTER TWO

THE taxi driver looked with curiosity at Amanda as she paid the fare. She knew she must look a sight; she had walked quite a distance in the heavy rain before hailing a taxi. She felt so cold that she was numb, and her fingers could barely grip her front door key as she turned it and entered the mews house which had been her home for the last couple of years.

She slipped off her wet shoes and her feet sank into the deep peach carpet. She should really have gone upstairs and taken her wet clothes off—the rain had penetrated their flimsy layers straight through to her underwear—only she didn't have the energy. Shock, and her intensity of emotion, had drained her strength. She padded through to the lounge, sank wearily into the floral-upholstered settee, and rested her head back against the soft feather cushions without giving a thought to how wet she would make them.

'God, what a mess!' she groaned out loud as she thought about that scene in her father's office—only it wasn't her father's office any more. Her eyes clouded with helpless tears. Drew had succeeded in taking away the one thing in her life that gave her a sense of purpose. It was calculated, of course; every move that man made was premeditated. He knew how important Hunter Fashions was to her. How he must be laughing at her now! She closed her eyes against the vision of his amused smile and mocking dark eyes, and hatred for him filled her tense body. The animosity she felt towards him was even stronger than it had been a year ago. They said that time healed all wounds, yet time had only served to feed her resentment towards him, and now the wound was bleeding. Her eyes opened. That was what he wanted,

18

wasn't it—for her to suffer? That was why he had bought the business. There could be no other reason.

A clock ticked away the seconds, and the silence which Amanda usually found refreshing was oppressive. She felt just as she had when Drew had gone out of her life the last time: desolate, frightened, alone. She had promised herself that she would never allow herself to feel like that again. How she wished she had never set eyes on Drew Sheldon!

It had been a cruel trick of fate that she had met him in the first place—she should never have been up in the Lake District that weekend. It had been an irate phone call from James that had made her travel up. James Reece was a top photographer. He loved his job and took it very seriously, which was probably why Amanda got on with him so well; she understood that professional pride of his that made him crave perfection, and she was well used to his temperamental outbursts. He had been shooting a layout of her summer collection, which was to be featured by a women's magazine, and nothing—according to James—had been going right. The make-up artist was dreadful, the hairdressers were lousy and the models were worse! On a wild impulse Amanda had gone up to see for herself.

She remembered thinking that at least the location for the photographs was right as she turned her car up the driveway to Glen Lea. It was a large country hotel, its stone walls covered with ivy, its mullioned windows looking down over landscaped gardens and the icy blue of Coniston Water.

James had been overjoyed to see her. 'Thank God you're here!' he had exclaimed dramatically. 'Have you seen what they've given me to work with?' He had spread his hands, indicating the models who were standing by the banks of the lake looking extremely cold.

Amanda had felt immediate sympathy for them. 'I'm not surprised they don't look their best, the wind cutting across here is bitter!'

A frown had marred James's blond, classical good looks. 'A professional won't let a little thing like the weather make any difference.'

Amanda had supposed he was right, but she still felt sorry for the girls shivering in their light summer dresses. But that was the way it was with fashion, everything was done at least a season in advance. In summer the girls suffered heat-stroke in fur coats, in winter they froze.

'We're way behind schedule, two girls are down with 'flu,' James had complained sharply. Then suddenly the frown had gone, replaced with a speculative look she was only too familiar with.

'Oh, no!' she had told him quickly before he could voice the question. 'No, James, I will not model for you.' She had stood in once before for him, and it was not an experience she cared to repeat.

'Just for one dress,' James had murmured persuasively. 'The white ballgown. It's the most outstanding dress of your collection, and you want it to be shown to its best, don't you?'

'But I'm not a professional model, James,' she had protested as he steered her towards the hotel.

'You're a born model, a natural.' The words hadn't been said just to flatter her, he had spoken the truth. Amanda was a photographer's dream: she had that rare combination of luminescent beauty and vivacity of character which shone through on every picture.

'My camera could have a love affair with you,' he had told her later, as she stood by the water's edge in a strapless white dress that was more suited to a tropical night in the Bahamas than a winter's day by Coniston Water.

She had stuck her tongue out cheekily. The statement was a little too close to the truth for her to dignify it with a serious answer. James had once told her that he was in love with her, and she had gently but firmly told him that the feelings were not reciprocated. Luckily the episode hadn't put a strain on their friendship; the words had just been forgotten as if they had never been spoken. Amanda was glad; she valued James's company. 'Tell your camera that it hasn't clicked with me. I'm tired and I'm cold—haven't you taken enough photos for one day?'

'All right, honey, just a couple more on the boating jetty and we'll be finished,' he had promised.

'Two more. That's it, then,' she had told him resolutely, before turning to negotiate the wooden boards over the choppy blue water.

'Turn there, honey. That's perfect,' James had yelled. 'No, don't shiver, look sexy.'

'I'm trying.' She had pushed an impatient hand through her autumn-gold hair, and it was then that she had noticed Drew.

He had been standing only a few feet away from her on the shore, watching her intently and looking very amused when he caught her eye. 'You look very sexy, but utterly ridiculous,' he had laughed.

James had shouted something about moving further back, but she had only been half listening. Her attention had been locked on the darkly handsome man in the thick Aran jumper and jeans. She had taken a step backwards and her high heels had twisted suddenly as she stumbled and fell over the edge into the icy water. Shock and cold had knocked the breath from her body and she'd floundered helplessly in the deep water. Then two strong arms were around her and someone had hauled her out.

For a moment she had lain stunned, her lashes dark against the marble white of her skin. Then firm lips had come down against the softness of hers and heat and life had flooded back through her veins. Her eyes had flickered open and she had looked directly into the darkest, most disturbing eyes she had ever seen.

'Are you all right?' His deep voice had sent shivers through her that were not entirely due to the cold.

'Yes.' She'd gazed up at the powerful contours of his face and the impressive width of his shoulders.

'Are you sure?' There was concern in his voice, but also something else, something that she responded to without even realising it.

'No.' Her voice had trembled slightly, yet she had smiled invitingly up at him. It had seemed the most natural thing in the world to meet his lips as he lowered his head. Her lips had clung and responded to the domination of his with an intensity which had frightened her. Even when his mouth left hers, the potency of that kiss had remained with her.

'You'll ruin that dress, Amanda.' James had been furious with her, his rough tone bringing awareness rushing back. She had just kissed a man with more passion than any other before and she didn't even know his name! A delicate flush had lit her face; she had been surprised by her behaviour, mortified. Yet the intoxicating feelings his gentle caress had stirred up had refused to die.

'To hell with the dress.' Drew had picked her up easily and set her on her feet. 'If you don't get out of it you'll catch pneumonia.'

She'd flinched as she tried to walk beside him, back to the hotel, and he'd cast a scrutinising eye down over the smooth curves of her body to which the white dress was now clinging damply and revealingly. 'Have you hurt yourself?'

'No, but my ankle is a little painful. I think I went over on it.' Before she had been able to say anything else he had swung her easily up into his arms, and carried her into the hotel.

Amanda had found herself trembling when he'd put her down outside her bedroom door. Drew had smiled at her, that lazy, amused smile which made her heart skip a beat. He must have realised what effect he was having on her, she had felt so gauche and obvious.

'Are you free this evening?' The question had taken her by surprise and she had stared at him, wary caution in her eyes. Did he think from the way she had reacted to him that she would be just an easy pick-up?

Drew had watched her face, reading her expression without difficulty. 'My intentions are strictly honourable,' he had teased. 'I was only suggesting we have dinner together. Seduction isn't on the menu.'

She had blushed self-consciously. 'Dinner would be lovely.'

Later, as she had been getting ready to meet him, James had come to her room. 'Don't get involved with him, Amanda,' he had warned.

'Why ever not?' Her eyes had met his in the mirror of her dressing-table and her hand had paused with a hairbrush in mid-air.

'You know who he is, don't you?' James frowned and continued, 'Drew Sheldon, the hotel magnate. He's in the gossip columns nearly every week, pictured with a different girl each time. The man is the worst ladykiller out.'

'We're only having dinner, James, don't be so stuffy.' Even as she'd said the words a curl of apprehension had stirred within her.

'Well, don't say I didn't warn you.'

She thought about those words now and shivered. Yes, she had been warned, but it hadn't made the slightest difference. She had still gone ahead, naïvely believing that Drew's feelings for her were different. At least her eyes had been opened while there was still time to rescue her pride from the debris. A bitter smile curved her lips. At least she hadn't been the complete walkover he had thought she would be.

The doorbell rang, bringing her back to the present with a jolt. Someone had their finger on the bell and wasn't lifting it. The shrill, insistent noise made her move quickly and angrily to open the door.

She felt a deep thrust of fear as she saw Drew standing outside, the collar of his heavy overcoat turned up against the rain, a dark, ominous look on his face.

'What are you doing here?' she asked breathlessly.

'That's the second time today you've asked me that,' he said acrimoniously. 'Aren't you going to invite me in?'

'No,' she said flatly. Over his shoulder she could see his limousine waiting for him, a long, black, gleaming monster which spoke volumes about his wealth and power. The sight of it aggravated her further. 'Go and intimidate some other defenceless person.' She started to close the door, but Drew's foot jammed it as he pushed easily into her hall.

'I can think of a lot of adjectives to describe you, Amanda, but defenceless isn't one of them. That tongue of yours is sharper than any deadly weapon.'

'I was referring to my father.' She glared at him, the door still open, waiting for him to leave. With one powerful thrust he knocked it out of her hand so that it slammed shut.

'So you do think about your father occasionally, then?' His voice was heavy with sarcasm. 'Judging from that display of temper you treated us to today, I didn't think you thought of anyone but yourself.'

'I love my father.' Her voice trembled with rage. 'I just happen to think he needs protecting from sharks like you.'

Drew's eyes rested on her pale face and fiery gold hair, which was curling in damp disarray, before sliding disparagingly down over her voluptuous figure accentuated by wet clothes. 'What a pity,' he drawled mockingly. 'You have the body of a beautiful woman and the mind of a spoilt child.'

A slow wave of humiliating colour swept over her. 'If you've finished insulting me, you can leave,' she said tightly.

'But I haven't finished, Amanda. I've only just started.' He moved away from her into the living-room and she had no option other than to follow him. 'You've redecorated, I see,' he observed with lazy interest.

For a moment she found herself looking at the room through his eyes. It was invitingly romantic: a Chinese rug covered the warm peach carpet, picking out the gentle peach and green shades of the scatter cushions on the two settees that were facing each other. Curtains which matched the floral upholstery of the settees framed the wide patio doors leading to the secluded garden.

'Nice,' Drew commented as he walked over to look more closely at a dreamy painting of a young boy and girl standing in a meadow of flowers.

'James bought that for me.' She was pleased to be able to tell him that; it made her feel more impervious towards him for some reason.

'Don't tell me that idiot is still around.'

'You were admiring his taste a few moments ago.' A small note of triumph entered her voice.

'His taste was never in question.' He turned to look at her, and his dark eyes seemed to burn straight through her, making her tremble. 'You should take those wet clothes off, I don't want you off work with 'flu.'

'I made it perfectly clear that I wouldn't be working for you,' she said scornfully.

'Maybe I didn't make it clear enough that you would.' There was cruel mockery in his voice. 'Your father told you I'd bought everything. Well, that included you, my darling.'

'Don't be ridiculous!' The trembling in her body seemed to have been transferred to her speech. 'You can't buy and sell people like unwanted possessions. We have a little thing called freedom in this country.'

'We also have little things called contracts,' he told her complacently, 'where you can sign away your life on a dotted line.'

'You're crazy!' Her voice wavered precariously.

He shrugged. 'Maybe. But I still own your contract, and I mean to collect what I paid for.'

Amanda could hear the heavy slam of her heartbeat filling her ears as fear and animosity jostled for position. 'This goes deeper than just business, doesn't it, Drew?' she said at last with a hiss of rage. 'What you're collecting is an old debt.'

'You do like to flatter yourself, don't you, Amanda?'

He sounded so self-assured that she itched to slap his face. 'Contract or not, I still won't work for you.'

'Then I'll sue you,' he told her calmly.

'You wouldn't dare!' The words flew out of her mouth before she could even think about them.

'Oh, wouldn't I? Just try me.' His dark eyes challenged her. 'I can see the headlines in the papers now—ex-fiancé sues for breach of contract.'

She stared at him, her eyes glimmering a deep jade. Was that what he wanted? Would that be his idea of the ultimate revenge? She shrugged, past caring. 'Go ahead, sue me. See if I care.'

'I wonder what your father will feel like when he reads about it in the newspapers?' Drew said quietly.

'You leave my father out of this!' Amanda rounded on him violently. 'Your vendetta is directed at me, not him.'

'What a strange, distorted view you have of me!' Drew moved closer towards her and she backed away. She felt curiously like an animal that was being manoeuvred into a corner ready for the kill. 'You're so wrapped up with your paranoia, you can't see reality.'

'What's that supposed to mean?' she snapped.

'Just that you haven't given one thought for your father in all this,' he said heavily.

'Of course I have.' She was instantly on the defensive. 'I know it wasn't in my father's best interests to sell the business to you. Seeing you wreck everything he's worked so hard for will destroy him.'

He ran an impatient hand through thick, dark hair. 'And if he stays on in the place it will kill him,' he said with cold finality.

All colour drained from Amanda's face. 'What do you mean?' Her throat felt dry and constricted.

'Haven't you stopped to wonder where he was this morning?' Drew's voice was gentler now.

She couldn't answer him, she could only stare at him with wide, panic-stricken eyes.

'He was at the doctor's, Amanda. Your father is retiring because he has to. He has a serious heart condition.'

The room seemed to sway and tilt around her; she could feel the floor rising up to meet her. Drew caught her as she crumpled down. Then oblivion mercifully blanked out the shock for a few short moments. Her eyes flickered open as Drew placed her gently on one of the settees and sat down beside her.

'I'm sorry I had to tell you like that,' he murmured. 'But your behaviour left me no choice.'

'I had no idea he was ill.' She looked up at him, too dazed by shock even to register how close he was to her. 'Why didn't he tell me?'

'I suppose he didn't want to worry you.'

Amanda closed her eyes. Yes, that would be the reason, it would be a typical reaction for her father. He was the type of person to want to shoulder the worry alone. It explained why he had been so insistent that she visit her mother for a holiday; he would have wanted her away so as not to cause her any anxiety.

'I should never have gone to Switzerland, I should have been here to help him,' she said almost to herself.

'You couldn't have done anything,' Drew said soothingly. 'All you can do is go along with his plans and give him no cause to worry.'

'Go along with *your* plans, you mean.' Her eyes flew open, wide and shimmering with tears.

'The two things do seem to coincide.' His lips twisted wryly.

'And if I refuse?'

His eyes narrowed on her. 'I told you. Then I drag your name through the courts.'

'Even though you know what that would do to my father?' She shook her head. 'I don't think you would do that, you both got on well. You liked each other.'

'There's no sentiment in business, Amanda,' Drew said in a deep, quiet voice. 'Call my bluff, and you'll be gambling with your father's life.'

Her eyes fixed on his harsh face, her body rigid and chilled. 'You really are a ruthless, cold-blooded swine!'

He acknowledged the insult, his mouth curving in a hard smile. 'It helps when you're dealing with someone who has ice in her veins.' He leaned closer, and she was suddenly aware of the strong pressure of his body next to hers. 'What happened to all that warmth that used to flow through you?' he asked softly.

She felt her body clench in sudden, incredible tension as he reached out a large hand and trailed it down the side of her face in a dangerously gentle caress.

'I channelled it towards somebody else.' She raised her hand to stave off his disturbing touch, and he caught it in an ironlike grip.

'That hurts!' she gasped, looking up to where her slim wrist was locked in a powerful hand that could have easily snapped it in half.

'Does it?'

She shivered at the impassive coldness of his tone. 'That's what all this is about, isn't it, Drew?' she demanded breathlessly. 'You're out to hurt me, to extract revenge because I rejected you for James.'

His mouth curved in a smile which didn't quite reach his eyes. 'That's really very funny. But I'm sorry to disappoint you, I'm not interested in yesterday's goods.' His eyes travelled down over the swell of her breasts with a look that made her shudder. 'You should take those clothes off, you're soaked through.' He released his hold on her, and before she could move his hand was touching her blouse. She could feel the heat from him radiate through the wet material, shaping the silken roundness of her breast. The feeling was electric. Wild tremors ran through her, and her heart beat so heavily, she was sure he could feel it slamming against his hand.

'Don't touch me, I hate it!' The panic-stricken words were out before she could check them.

The smile hardened on his mouth. 'Why are you behaving like an outraged little virgin, Amanda, when we both know you're anything but?' His fingers stroked sensually, setting her body alight with excitement. Against her will she could feel every nerve in her body responding to his touch.

He bent his head closer; she could smell the familiar aroma of his aftershave, and feel his cool breath against her skin. For one heart-stopping moment she thought he was going to kiss her. Instead he pulled back from her, his hands leaving her body.

She stared at the cold light in his eyes, bewildered by the conflicting emotions tearing her apart.

'You're the one who's hung up on the past, Amanda,' he said harshly. 'You still want me as much as you did a year ago in the Lake District.'

'No!' The word was torn from her. 'No, I hate you, I can't stand you anywhere near me!' Drew laughed, and it was a cold, mirthless sound. 'Hate is a very strong emotion; are you sure you're deciphering it correctly?'

'I thought I made my feelings for you clear when I broke our engagement.' Her voice trembled betrayingly.

'Your feelings seem to blow hot and cold with the weather.' He got to his feet and stared down at her. 'My reasons for buying Hunter Fashions are purely business ones, so I suggest you get those irrational ideas out of your mind and report to work tomorrow.'

She climbed stiffly to her feet and glared at him. 'I don't care what your reasons for buying the business are. The fact still remains that I don't want to work for you under any circumstances.'

'Fine.' He shrugged as if he couldn't care less what she did, and glanced at his watch. 'I've wasted enough time on you. If you don't report in at nine tomorrow then I will instruct my solicitor to act accordingly.' He turned his back on her and moved towards the front door. 'I gather you don't care what effect this will have on your father.'

'You know damn well I do!' She followed him angrily.

'Well, then, you will have to think very carefully about your actions,' he said grimly.

Their glances locked like two enemies in mortal combat. 'What you're doing is emotional blackmail,' she accused him.

'I'm well aware of what I'm doing,' he said drily.

Amanda hated him so much, it hurt. Her hands balled into tight fists and she longed to fly at him and tear great lumps out of his cool, self-satisfied face.

The doorbell rang beside her, making her jump and snatch the door open angrily. 'Yes?' She barked the word without even looking to see who it was.

'No need to bite my head off. I only called to say welcome home,' a familiar voice drawled.

Amanda's eyes focused dazedly on James's handsome face.

CHAPTER THREE

'WELL, aren't you going to invite me in? I'm getting wet out here.' From the wide smile on James's face it was obvious he hadn't noticed Drew standing back in the shadows of the hall.

'I'm sorry, James, come on in.' Amanda stepped back to allow him to enter, but instead of passing her he wrapped her in a warm embrace.

'It's good to have you home, honey, it really is,' he whispered in her ear. 'I can't tell you how much I missed you.' He moved back and looked at her critically. 'Hey, you're all wet!'

'So are you.' She smiled, more than a little uncomfortable and very conscious of Drew standing behind James. She could see the mocking gleam in his dark eyes as he watched them, and for some reason it made her even more flustered. 'I missed you, too.' She brushed a drop of imaginary moisture from the side of his face. Even as she made the gesture she knew she was only doing it for Drew's benefit.

James flushed bright pink in surprise and pleasure at the uncharacteristic show of affection.

'I've brought some wine.' He held up the bottle wrapped with a big red bow. 'Let's crack it open and celebrate.'

'What a good idea,' Drew said in a dry, amused voice.

The colour drained from James's face as he turned to look incredulously at the man behind him.

'Hello, Reece.' A smile curled Drew's lips; it was a smile which looked dangerously like a sneer.

'Sheldon.' The name sounded vaguely insulting on James's lips.

For a moment the air was filled with tension. Amanda remembered the last time the two men had met and she shivered; that scene had been like some horrible nightmare. She didn't want to think about it, not now, when she needed to have all her wits about her.

James stroked his jawline thoughtfully and she wondered if he also was remembering that night and the way Drew had hit him, so forcefully and with such brutal strength that he had sent him sprawling over her living-room like a rag doll.

Drew reached out lazily and took the bottle he was holding in a nerveless grasp. He pursed his lips thoughtfully as he studied the label. 'Not the best year, but it will do for a lunch-time drink.' He looked over at Amanda with cool, dark eyes. 'You'd better go and put some dry clothes on. I'll do the honours with the drink.'

Amanda glared angrily at him; the man had a real cheek! 'Haven't you got an appointment with your accountant?' she asked pointedly.

He glanced at his watch. 'Jordan will have gone for lunch now, which reminds me, I'm quite hungry myself. Any chance of some food to go with the wine?'

'No, there is no chance whatsoever,' she answered sharply. 'I have no food in the house.'

Drew shook his head in mock admonition. 'No wonder you're looking so scrawny these days! You should eat properly, Amanda. You can't do your best at work if you're undernourished.'

The withering look she sent him from jade-green eyes plainly told him to go to hell. Her animosity only seemed to make him look more amused. 'You run along and slip into something more comfortable. James and I can have a little talk while we wait for you.'

Amanda's eyes widened at the disconcerting idea of leaving the two men alone to talk, but before she could argue he returned to the living-room, leaving James staring after his broad back in confusion.

'What the hell is he doing here?' he hissed in a low voice.

'I don't really know,' she said in a distracted tone. 'It seems that he's bought my father's business.'

'What?' James turned, his voice rising with incredulity. 'What the blazes does he want with a fashion house?'

'Ssh!' Amanda warned nervously. 'He'll hear you.' She moved quickly towards the stairs. 'I don't know what his reasons are. Why don't you go in there and ask him? Maybe you'll be able to make some sense out of it.'

'Don't worry, I will.' James moved into the living-room, his face set in a grim line. He looked just like a small boy about to enter the lion's den, Amanda thought with a feeling of unease.

Once inside her bedroom, she lost no time in getting changed. She opened her wardrobe and took out the first appropriate clothes that came to hand—a pair of faded, stonewashed jeans and a blue cashmere jumper. The idea of having a hot shower ran briefly through her mind, but she dismissed it quickly. She didn't want to leave the two men alone together. What would they be discussing?

Her hands trembled as she unzipped her skirt and took off her blouse and jacket. For a moment she stared at her reflection in the mirrored wardrobe door, as she took her lacy underwear off. Did Drew really think that she looked scrawny? She had lost a little weight since she'd known him, but her slender figure was still curvy, her breasts full and rounded. Unwanted, the memory of his hands against her skin crept into her mind, making her body burn alarmingly as if some fever had struck it.

She turned away, impatient and angry with herself. She didn't care what Drew thought of her body, she hated him and she wanted him nowhere near her. She towel-dried her hair with ferocious vigour, flung on her jeans and jumper and raced down the stairs.

James was standing with his back towards the window. He looked strained, a glass of wine clutched in a tense hand. Drew, however, was completely relaxed, lounging back in one of the settees, his long legs stretched lazily out in front of him.

'Ah, Amanda,' his dark eyes roamed over her flushed skin and tousled gold hair, 'I've poured you a glass of wine.' He indicated her glass sitting next to his on the coffee-table.

She moved to pick it up, but didn't sit beside him; instead she stood next to James as if for moral support.

'Now, what shall we drink to?' Drew enquired, and then, before either could answer him, he went on, 'How about to happy reunions?' He lifted his glass and drank deeply of the golden liquid, seemingly unaware that neither one of them joined him.

'Are you kept busy at work these days, Reece?' Drew looked over at them, his lazy air of satisfaction and the insouciant question making Amanda's nerves jump.

'I'm always busy, as a matter of fact I have some work lined up at Hunters for next month——' His voice trailed off as realisation of what that would mean dawned on him.

'So you're going to be part of our happy team.' Drew eyed them both with distinct mockery. 'Perhaps we should be drinking to my good fortune in acquiring two such talented employees.' He lifted his glass. 'Here's to a long and rewarding association.'

'Rewarding for whom, I wonder,' Amanda said in a dry voice.

Drew drained his glass and stood up. 'That remains to be seen,' he said derisively. 'If my staff please me I can be a very agreeable and generous employer; if they don't——' He gave a shrug and his voice trailed off ominously, making Amanda shudder. 'I'll leave you both to your celebrations.' Drew moved towards the door, his movements supple, the muscled power of a tiger rippling beneath his expensive suit. 'I'll see you both in the office, no doubt.' He stopped and turned by the door. 'Don't forget about the little party your father is throwing for me at the weekend, Amanda. I'm sure you'll want to come along and welcome me properly.'

Before she could answer, he had gone, leaving behind the lingering, faint aroma of aftershave. Amanda flinched as the front door closed with quiet resolution, her nerves stretched to breaking point. For a moment there was a stunned silence in the room. This must be what a fly would feel like, trapped in a scheming spider's web, she thought with a shiver of fear. Drew was playing some deadly game with her, enjoying her distress. What was his objective? She couldn't believe that buying Hunter Fashions was just a business move on his part; the man was calculating, and he never made a move unless he had a target well in view.

'What is he playing at?' Her voice came out in a strained whisper, and she didn't even realise that she had spoken out loud until James answered her.

'That, my dear, is blatantly obvious.' He put down his wine and crossed the room towards the glass drinks cabinet. 'Do you mind if I help myself to something stronger?'

Amanda shook her head and watched as he poured himself a Scotch. 'What do you mean, it's obvious? Did he say anything while I was upstairs?'

'I'll tell you what he said.' James sat down on one of the settees and stared at her with piercing blue eyes. 'He asked me why you hadn't married me yet.'

The blood drained from Amanda's face and she moved to sit down on the settee facing him. 'Maybe he just asked out of polite interest,' she suggested, although deep down she knew there was more to it than that.

'Oh, it was all said in a jovial man-to-man tone, but underneath he was weighing me up in that astute, cool way of his.' He took a deep drink. 'Did you notice how he was watching us as he sat here? He was interrogating us.'

'What did you say to him?' She ran a trembling hand through the length of her hair.

'I told him we were too busy with our respective careers for marriage,' James answered starkly.

'That's all right, then.' Amanda leaned back into the settee and took a sip of wine.

'Oh, for God's sake, Amanda, the man's not stupid!' James exploded. 'He'll know there's no reason why we can't get married and also keep our careers.'

'Maybe he's not all that bothered what we do.' Amanda was desperately trying to keep rational. 'After all, he's a very busy man and he has lots of women in his life. Why should it matter to him what I do? He was never very interested in me in the first place.'

'Don't be silly, Amanda.' James looked scornfully at her. 'You were Drew Sheldon's possession, his ring was on your finger. The fact that he didn't love you doesn't make any difference to him.'

Amanda flinched visibly. 'I don't want to talk about this, James. It's in the past, dead and buried.'

'No, it's not.' He shook his head, his pale brows coming together in a frown. 'When you broke your engagement with Sheldon you offended him bitterly. When you told him you were in love with me, you rubbed his already bruised ego raw. Now he's out to make us pay for the humiliation we inflicted on him '

She sat there, frozen on the spot. It was terrifying, hearing all the fears that were racing around inside her voiced aloud. 'I should never have involved you in this, James,' she said at last. 'I used you like some weapon against him, and it was very wrong of me.'

'Oh, honey!' James groaned and came to sit beside her. 'You're not the guilty one in all this. The blame rests squarely at Sheldon's door. He was the one who was dishonest.'

'Yes, but by lying to him about us I made myself as guilty as he is,' Amanda said bitterly.

'And what were you supposed to do? Let him wipe his feet on you as well?' James demanded angrily. 'For heaven's sake, the man was running around with every

beautiful woman in town—and then some,' he finished
heavily.

Amanda got shakily to her feet. Yes, Drew had tried
to make a fool of her, and she had been justified in
striking back at him, even though it had hurt at the
time—God, how it had hurt! She had tried to wipe the
whole distressing episode out of her mind, but she had
never really succeeded; it was always there at the back
of her thoughts, colouring her every move.

Drew was the reason why she buried herself so much
in her work, why she had no wish to get into a serious
relationship with any of the men who asked her out.

'Amanda.' James's voice interrupted her musing.
'You'll have to start looking for another job.'

'What?' She stared at him blankly for a moment before
shaking her head. 'No—I can't.'

'You are not working for Drew Sheldon. I won't allow
it.' It was an angry, proprietorial command. He had
never spoken to her like that before. She was surprised
and annoyed at his manner.

'You're my friend, James, not my keeper.' She said
the words quietly but there was an icy warning note in
them. Immediately his angry countenance was replaced
by one of brooding hurt.

'I'm only trying to help you,' he assuaged. 'God,
Amanda, have you forgotten how that man hurt you,
tore you apart? I don't want to see that happen to you
again.'

'He can't do that to me again because I don't care
about him any more.' The words felt stiff in her mouth,
as if her brain had formed them but her body rejected
them. She looked remorsefully over at James; she
shouldn't have snapped at him like that. He had been a
good friend to her over the last year, had helped her
through some rough times. He was only concerned for
her. If only she could have fallen in love with someone
like him, life would be so much simpler. 'I don't want

to work for Drew,' she assured him. 'But for the time being I'm going to have to.'

'You don't have to do anything you don't want to do.' He ran an impatient hand through thick blond hair. 'Did you notice that satisfied gleam in Sheldon's eyes when he asked me what I was doing workwise? He knew damn well I had some lined up at Hunter's next month. He's revelling in his power over us; you can't give him the satisfaction of holding on to that.'

'I'm going to have to.' She held up a hand as James looked set to interrupt her. 'It's different for you, James, you work as a freelance photographer. All you need do is tell him you're too busy to do any work for him. I've just signed a two-year contract.'

'So break it,' said James grimly.

'I wish I could.' She took a deep, steadying breath. 'But I've got my father to consider, and at the moment his wellbeing comes first.' She looked at James and her green eyes misted with tears. 'He's not well; I'm so worried about him. I don't think he would be strong enough to cope with the trauma my breaking my contract would bring.'

'Well, he should have thought about that before he sold the business to your ex-fiancé,' James said roughly.

'I can't believe you just said that!' Amanda stared at him. 'My father has a serious heart condition and all you can do is gripe about who he sold out to.'

'I didn't mean it like that.' James got hurriedly to his feet and came around the settee to stand next to her. 'I'm just so concerned for you. You're in such a vulnerable situation, and I can't stand to see you get hurt.' He put a tentative arm around the stiffness of her shoulders.

Amanda allowed herself to relax against him for a moment, closing her eyes wearily. 'I'm sorry, James, I know you mean well. I don't know why I'm so edgy.'

'That's all right, sweetheart,' he soothed. 'It's under-standable. I'll help you sort everything out; you shouldn't have much problem breaking your contract.'

Amanda shook her head, suddenly realising that, much as she detested the thought of working for Drew, there was no way she was going to risk upsetting her father. 'No, James, I've made up my mind, I'm going to work for Drew for the time being.'

She could feel his body tense. 'Well, that's your pre-rogative,' he said dully. 'But don't say I didn't warn you, just as I did last time.'

'This time it's different,' Amanda insisted. 'My re-lationship with Drew will be just a business one; there's no way he can hurt me.'

'If you say so,' James said drily.

'I do.' Amanda broke away from him, gathering herself together. 'I think I should go and see my father; I behaved pretty badly this morning and he looked dreadful when I left.'

'I'll give you a lift.'

Amanda shook her head. 'Thanks all the same, but I—I'd like to be alone for a while.'

James watched thoughtfully as she picked up the empty glasses from the table. 'I'll go, then.'

'Yes.' She watched as he walked towards the door. 'Thank you for being concerned about me, James,' she said softly.

He hesitated for a moment. 'That's all right. I guess someone has to be around to pick up the pieces.'

As soon as the door closed behind him Amanda sank down into the settee, his words lingering in her ears, mocking her. Drew doesn't have the power to hurt me any more, she told herself firmly. Everything would be all right. But would it? a little voice asked inside. She had wanted James to go so that she could gather herself together before facing her father; she didn't want him or anyone else to guess just how terrified she was by Drew's sudden reappearance into her life.

The phone rang beside her and she reached automatically to answer it, surprised by her father's clear, firm voice.

'Amanda, are you all right?'

She swallowed on a sudden lump in her throat. 'Don't you think it should be me asking that question?' she asked gently.

There was a heavy silence for a moment. 'Drew told you, then?' he said at last.

'I don't think I left him any option.' She found herself defending Drew and immediately felt flustered.

'I can imagine.' There was a note of amusement in her father's voice now. 'You always did have a temper to match that fiery hair of yours.'

'I'm sorry about this morning—I shouldn't have said those...'

'There's no need to apologise, Amanda,' he cut in sharply. 'I know it all must have come as a great shock to you.'

'The biggest shock was hearing that you...' she floundered, unable to bring herself to voice the words.

'That I have a heart condition,' he finished for her flatly. 'I didn't tell you because I don't want you running around after me as if I'm some sort of invalid. All I need is to take things easy and rest—I'll be fine.'

'All the same, I think I should ring Mum and...'

'No!' The word was sharp and loud. 'When are you going to get it through your head that we're divorced, Amanda, and we're never going to get back together.' The words echoed back down the years and Amanda swallowed and closed her eyes, remembering how he had said those exact same words to her when she was thirteen, only then he had tacked on, 'People change, love doesn't always last for ever.' They were words that had stayed with her, burnt on her memory.

'I just thought it might help,' she said quietly.

'Well, it wouldn't.' His voice was softer now. 'Look, Amanda, the best thing you can do for me is continue as normal. Co-operate with Sheldon; he's a good man and he can do a lot more for your career than I ever could.'

'Somehow my career doesn't seem that important any more.'

'Well, it's important to me,' her father answered drily.

'I know.' Amanda took a deep breath. 'That's why I've decided to stay on at Hunter's—just for a short while to see how things go.'

'Good girl.' The relief in her father's voice was evident. 'I knew you would be sensible about things. I'll see you up at the house on Friday night for the welcome party, then?'

'I—I suppose so.' Amanda closed her eyes and thought how ludicrous life could be. It was absurd attending a welcome party for the one man she wished was a million miles away.

Amanda couldn't sleep that night. She lay staring into the darkness, shadows of the past haunting her. Drew smiling at her, Drew making her laugh, Drew kissing her. Scenes which she only wanted to bury flashed inside her mind like light bulbs being suddenly switched on, cruelly illuminating every feature of his face, every wonderful moment.

A week was all they had had together in the Lakes. The most beautiful, idyllic week of her life. It had pleased her to think that Drew had come to the north of England on business and yet had attended to none of it because of her. They had spent every day together, and with every passing moment Amanda had felt herself drawn more deeply to him. On their first date, Drew had kissed her tenderly; on the second his kisses had grown more demanding and intense. She had no doubts that if she had been a different type of girl she would have been in bed with him that night, but Drew had come up against a barrier that he hadn't expected and certainly wasn't accustomed to. Amanda had never slept with any of the

young men she had dated, she had never wanted to, never
felt her blood turn to fire as it did when she was in Drew's
arms. She had pulled back from him, wariness in her
eyes. She had been warned about his reputation with
women and she didn't want to be just one more conquest on his list. Drew hadn't pushed her, and that fact
had made her fall more deeply under his spell.

Drew had been so charming, handsome, witty. They
had talked for hours, laughed at the most absurd things
and walked hand in hand, happy just being in each
other's company. He had been all she had ever dreamed
about in a man and, when he touched her, her heart had
pounded and her senses had become wildly aware of his
every movement.

On their last evening, he had taken her into his arms
and she had melted against him. She had desperately
wanted to look up at him and say, 'Yes, please, I want
to...' But she just couldn't. She had been so afraid that
if she gave in to her desires she would lose him, that he
would sleep with her and then move on to the next conquest. She had hated herself, and as the silent battle raged
inside her he had put her firmly away from him.

'I have to go back to London tomorrow,' he had said
softly. Her heart had swooped despairingly at those
words, but she had remained silent. 'I'll phone you and
we'll go out some time.'

She had nodded bravely, her green eyes glimmering
brightly in the dull light of evening. 'That would be
lovely.' Remarkably, her voice had been steady, with no
hint of the tears that threatened to flow at any minute.
As she watched him walk away from her, she had been
convinced that she would never see him again.

She had found returning to work difficult, to say the
least. She couldn't concentrate on anything, she wasn't
interested in anything. All she could think about was
Drew; she had found herself wishing that she had slept
with him, and then despised herself for her weak

thoughts. Wouldn't she be in a far worse state if she had?

Two miserable weeks had passed, when she couldn't eat or sleep. Then one evening she had opened up her door and he had been standing outside. He had smiled that lazy, charming smile. 'I would have come sooner, but I've been tied up with a backlog of work.'

Her heart had thumped like crazy against her ribs and her legs had suddenly felt like water, but she had smiled calmly. 'That's all right, come in.'

'I was hoping you would have dinner with me tonight, or have you got other plans?' he'd asked smoothly.

She had hesitated; she had made no arrangements for the evening, but perhaps she shouldn't act as if she were easily available. After all, he had made no move to contact her in a full fortnight. She hadn't wanted him to think she'd been anxiously sitting waiting for him. She had looked up into his dark eyes and suddenly the refusal had died and she had found herself telling him that she had no other plans.

'Good.' He had smiled and her fate had been sealed.

He had taken her to an expensive restaurant, where they served only the best food and wine. It had been wasted on Amanda that evening, for she was too busy studying Drew's handsome face in the intimate glow of the candlelight.

'I missed you, Amanda.' His voice had been deep and sensuous and had sent tingles of anticipation running down her spine.

'I missed you too,' she had admitted breathlessly. He'd stretched out a hand across the table and taken her small hand in his. All her reservations towards him had crumbled at that caress. She had known that tonight there would be no way she would be able or would want to keep him outside her bedroom door. Strange that he had chosen that precise moment when she had lowered her barriers against him anyway to propose marriage. If he had known what was running through her mind he would never have asked her; hadn't he admitted as much during a bitter argument later? But she had been naïvely unaware of his motives. She had really believed at that moment that he loved her, though he had never uttered the word once; even when he made passionate love to her afterwards, that word had never been spoken.

Incredibly, she hadn't given that fact a thought at the time. She had been too wrapped up by her own feelings for him. She had been thinking all those crazy thoughts that went through a woman's brain when she fell for someone. She remembered lying cradled in his arms, wishing that the night could last for ever, and then feeling a wave of happiness wash over her as she thought about spending the rest of her life with him. It was only when the morning came, and he left her bed, that the first doubts had crept in...

She reached out a hand and switched on the bedside lamp. The bright golden light dimmed the memory. For a moment she lay still while her eyes adjusted to the glare, and roughly she brushed a tear away.

'You're letting him do it to you again,' she whispered into the silence. 'You're allowing him to get to you, to upset you.' She looked at the clock—it was only three a.m. She felt as if it should at least be eight. She sighed and threw the covers on the bed back. Perhaps some cocoa would help calm her.

She looked at herself in the large mirror on the wardrobe door as she put her dressing-gown on. Her skin was deathly white, her eyes dark and enormous. She looked washed out, even the dramatic flame-coloured hair which tumbled over her shoulders making little difference to her pallor.

'Why are you letting that man spoil your beauty sleep?' she asked her reflection crossly. 'You got over him long ago.' The words hung heavily in the silence, her reflection stared back at her ironically. You're not completely immune, it seemed to mock, otherwise you wouldn't look the way you do, the way you used to when things were going wrong between you.

Two months, that was how long their engagement had lasted, and with every passing day her doubts had grown. They had only seen each other on five occasions during that time, and Drew had broken more dates with her than he had kept. When she was with him she was able to justify that to herself; she could understand that work claimed a large proportion of Drew's time. He had hotels scattered far and wide around the world—of course he had to leave the country to attend to them. She was able to accept those facts when she was lying in his arms. It was when he was gone and she opened up the paper and saw photographs of him attending functions and meetings and saw the number of beautiful women who were constantly by his side that she started to view him in a different light. Oh, it was never flagrantly stated that he was having affairs, and at first she was so naïve she hadn't even read between the lines. It was only when it was bluntly drawn to her attention that she had stopped to think about it. Or perhaps she had known all along and just hadn't been able to face the truth until she had overheard that conversation between some of her friends. Amanda's mouth twisted wryly as she thought about Kezia Van Slyke and her illustrious cronies, who were always to be found at the 'best' parties and gatherings. Using the word 'friend' to describe any of them, was being over-generous. They were like a hungry pack of wolves, eyeing everyone carefully, criticism and scandal rich on their tongues.

Usually Amanda didn't listen to their snide vicious-ness, but when she had heard them mention Drew she had been compelled against all her better judgement to stand and hear what they had to say. Perhaps if she had been in a better frame of mind she never would have bothered, but she had been at a low ebb to start with. Drew should have attended that party with her, only he had rung earlier to say he was unavoidably detained in Paris.

'I see Drew Sheldon is conspicuous by his absence.' Kezia Van Slyke's sharp voice had carried clearly above the noise of the party, causing quite a few interested heads to turn. 'Poor Amanda, I don't think she realises yet that women have to stand in line for Drew.'

Amanda had shifted uncomfortably and tried to look as if she was listening to the young couple who were talking to her.

'I bumped into him at the airport only a few days ago with the most beautiful blonde clinging to his side. He said he was off on business,' Kezia added with heavy sarcastic implication and then laughed. 'Darling Drew, I don't think he will ever change.'

Amanda tried not to notice the sympathetic looks a few people around her were sending. That they should feel pity for her was just the last straw; only a fool needed pity, and she certainly wasn't that. She tried to tell herself that it was just malicious gossip, that no one in their right mind would listen to Kezia. Then she started to wonder about the mysterious blonde. Drew had never mentioned that anyone was accompanying him on his trips abroad. Perhaps the whole incident was a figment of Kezia Van Slyke's fertile imagination?

After a sleepless night, Amanda had decided to confront Drew with her fears that very morning. His plane should have touched down in London at five a.m., so she waited until eight and then went over to his private suite at the Sheldon Hotel where he stayed when he was in London, except for the last few occasions when he had stayed with Amanda.

Her body trembled now as she recalled that nightmare of a morning. The confident way she had told the man on the desk that she was Drew Sheldon's fiancée before stepping smartly into the private lift. The poor man had looked slightly startled and she had got the distinct impression that he would have stopped her from going up if she hadn't moved so quickly. No wonder he had looked taken aback; he must have known. It seemed to Amanda that everyone had known except her.

She had felt incredibly foolish as she stood outside Drew's door and waited for him, almost like some stranger who didn't know Drew at all and had no right to be there. When the door had opened those feelings had intensified a million times, as she'd stared into the cold blue eyes of a very attractive blonde.

She was wearing a black, expensive-looking négligé which left little of her voluptuous, exquisite figure to the imagination. Her honey-blonde hair fell to her waist in seductive disarray.

'Who are you?' she had demanded harshly.

'I was about to ask you the same question,' Amanda had said quietly.

For a moment there had been silence, then comprehension had dawned in the woman's ice-blue eyes and she had smiled, a deriding, jeering smile. 'You must be Drew's little fiancée,' she had mocked. 'Don't look so surprised, he told me all about you.'

Amanda had been rooted to the spot, stunned with a shock that held her paralysed.

'Or maybe it's me you're surprised at. Ah, I can see it is,' the woman drawled. 'Well, I'm sorry if I shock you, but Drew doesn't live the life of a hermit, you know, and he doesn't need to put a ring on my finger in order to get *me* into bed.' Her words had been bitter, unmerciful. They had brought heat flowing back into Amanda's stunned body, the white-hot heat of anger and humiliation.

'Tell him I'm here and I want to see him,' she had demanded in a low, steady voice.

Pale eyebrows had risen slightly in surprise. 'At this precise moment, you're the last person Drew would want to see. Why don't you phone and leave a message on his answering machine, it will save you a lot of embar-

CHAPTER FOUR

AMANDA poured herself another cup of coffee and brought it back with her into her studio. She had given up trying to sleep hours ago, and it had been a relief to channel her thoughts into work. Amanda loved the joy of creating new and exciting designs, and the moment she lifted the cover off her desk her mind was immediately transported away from the heartache of remembering.

Dawn had broken without her even being aware of it, and now time was creeping inexorably towards the hour when she should leave for the office. Amanda switched off the powerful lamp on her desk and the cold grey light of morning filled the room. Her study was bright and airy, perfect for working in. She spent most of her time in this room, preferring it to her office at Hunter's. One wall was completely taken up with a sliding glass door which she left open in summer. Heavy rain pounded against it today, blurring the garden into a mass of jumbled colours. The streaming rivulets reflected over the white walls and shelves neatly stacked with her reference books and files on her previous designs. The weather, she thought, echoed her mood perfectly.

She sighed and looked down at her designs. She was working on a particularly lovely collection at the moment: bridal gowns and romantic dresses for trousseaux. She had just about finished it—or had she? Her eyes veered towards the side of her desk where some sheets of paper were separated from the rest. They were the designs for a very spectacular dress, one that was very special to Amanda, for she had designed it for herself, for her wedding to Drew.

She had decided weeks ago that she would include the dress in her collection; after all, she would never wear it, and it was a crime to keep such a superlative design on a shelf gathering dust. It seemed the sensible thing to do when she had thought she would be handing it over to her father, but now she wasn't so sure.

The dress had been designed with love. Every detail about it was special, inspired by the anticipation of wearing it for Drew. The thought of handing it over as part of a business deal made her hurt unbelievably inside. The rain reflected over the pristine white paper like tears, Amanda thought absently. Immediately the thought crossed her mind her mouth twisted scornfully—wasn't she the fool who had shed them? Decisively she reached for the designs and placed them all in her leather briefcase. She had no more tears left for Drew Sheldon and no more sentiment. This was business, pure and simple.

Amanda was on the last minute of her nine o'clock deadline when she arrived at the office, because, ridiculously, she hadn't been able to make up her mind what to wear.

She had tried on several outfits and then torn them all off and stared at herself with frustration in the mirror. For a woman who usually wore her clothes with casual ease, this was ludicrous! Finally she had reached into the back of her wardrobe and selected the plainest, most serious suit she possessed. It was a dark navy blue in colour, with a high collar and a straight skirt. On the rare occasions when she had worn it before, she had lightened the severity by clever use of accessories.

Today she made no concession to her femininity. She wore no jewellery, her shoes and handbag were workaday black and her hair was pulled severely back from her face into a topknot of gleaming copper.

'Good morning, Miss Hunter.' Sandy got up from her desk and took Amanda's coat. 'Mr Sheldon has called a meeting in the boardroom this morning. He asked for you to go straight in when you arrived.'

Amanda nodded and retraced her steps down the corridor. It seemed Drew had no doubts that she would turn up for work today. The thought that he was able to manipulate her so easily was maddening. Well, she wasn't going to put up with it for long, she told herself reassuringly. As soon as her father was looking stronger she would find a way to break her contract with Hunter Fashions.

She hesitated outside the boardroom. The thought of coming face to face with Drew made her stomach churn nervously. She glanced in the large gilded mirror beside the door and hardly recognised the tailored, austere young woman who looked back. She needed the confidence of this new crisp, businesslike look, needed it to hide behind. Drew might have won the battle over her working for him, but the war had only just begun.

She met the full impact of his dark eyes the moment she opened the door. His gaze slid assessingly over her as if he could see right through the severity of her clothes to the frivolous lace underwear beneath.

'So glad you decided to join us, Amanda.' His voice held a gleam of satisfaction which made her bristle with anger. Aware that all the senior members of staff were seated at the long, polished table, she forced herself to smile coolly and make no reply to that.

'Good morning, gentlemen.' She pointedly avoided Drew as she looked around at the other men, and took a spare seat as far away from him as possible.

She had only just sat down when the door opened behind her. Drew looked up and smiled. 'Ah, Jordan, come in.' Amanda turned and her whole body seemed to freeze as her eyes rested on the blue-eyed blonde who had entered. It was the woman who had smiled so scathingly at her over a year ago—the woman Drew had been sleeping with!

'I'm sorry I'm a little late, Drew, but I got held up in traffic.' Her voice was low and silky as she moved towards the head of the table and the spare seat at Drew's right-hand side.

She was wearing a magnificent pale blue suit which accentuated her slender yet voluptuous figure as she moved.

'That's all right, Jordan, we hadn't got down to business yet,' Drew said smoothly. 'Everyone, I would like to introduce you to Miss Jordan Lee, my accountant. Jordan will be working closely with us over the next couple of weeks, and she's coming in to do a complete audit of the books.'

Jordan's blue eyes flicked over the men at the table before coming to rest on Amanda, and there was the same look in their cool blue depths as there had been all that time ago when she had opened the door of Drew's private suite and made it clear exactly what their relationship was.

Amanda remained outwardly calm and composed, but inside she was seething with rage as she watched the two of them seated at the head of the table. If someone had told her a few days ago that she would be sitting at a meeting in Hunter Fashions chaired by Drew and his mistress, she would have told them they were crazy. Yet here she was, having to smile and look as if she didn't mind in the least.

'Now that all the introductions have been made, we can get down to the serious business of work.' Drew passed some folders down the table for each member of staff. When Amanda received hers she opened it and tried to focus her attention on the printed pages, but she didn't seem able to concentrate. Instead she found her eyes wandering towards the woman at Drew's side.

She looked more like a glossy film actress than an accountant. Her long blonde hair was caught on top of her head in large combs, allowing a few long stray tendrils to curl softly around her oval face. Her make-up was perfect, a faint hint of peach on her high cheek-bones, a deep russet on her full lips. Amanda found herself regretting her own style of dress. Compared to the other woman she felt dowdy and plain. The moment the thought crossed her mind she was annoyed with herself. She wasn't in competition with Jordan; as far as she was concerned Drew could sleep with her plus the entire female staff—she didn't give a damn.

'As you can see,' Drew was saying incisively, 'my aim is to turn Hunter Fashions into a worldwide name. I want it to be as well known in Paris, New York and Rome as it is in London. And I plan to more than treble its profits within the first twelve months. Jordan will be drawing up some target figures for us to work towards.' He directed a smile towards the other woman which Amanda found totally nauseating.

She glanced around at the men seated at the burnished mahogany table, studying the plans Drew had placed before them. They were all employees who had worked for her father for years, good, trustworthy men who had helped to build the fashion house up out of nothing. She wondered what they would make of Drew's ideas. Would they resent him? He was, after all, a good deal younger than them all.

Recalcitrantly she hoped they would. What did Drew know about the fashion business, anyway? How dared he sit in here and dictate to people who had dedicated their whole lives to the industry?

She focused her attention on Drew and listened to what he was saying. After only a few short moments one thing was very clear, and that was that Drew had done his homework; he knew exactly what he was doing. As much as she disliked him, she had to grudgingly admit he was a brilliant businessman.

He controlled the meeting effortlessly. Any problems the men voiced were dealt with with a masterly competence, which soon had all of them filled with enthusiasm for his ideas.

Strangely, their obvious respect and admiration for him only seemed to irritate Amanda more. He was so calm and confident, so utterly attractive in his dark grey business suit. His eyes were dark and serious as he answered a question someone put to him, his mouth firm. He was used to people's deference to his ideas. He was a man who commanded respect and always received it. He made Amanda want to stand up and say, 'I disagree.' Just for the hell of it.

'Well, Amanda, you've been very quiet.' Drew turned to meet her eyes as if he was well aware of what was going through her mind. 'What do you think about the new proposals for Hunter Fashions?' His eyes glittered as if he dared her to condemn them.

'They sound wonderful.' There was more than a trace of scepticism in her voice. 'But just how are you going to achieve such remarkable results in such a short space of time? We've all been working for years towards the targets you're outlining.'

'The idea is a very simple one. I'm going to place a boutique in each of my hotels, starting with the Paris Sheldon where work is already under way.'

There was an immediate buzz of excitement around the table. 'I see.' Amanda looked away from him. It was the most obvious thing to do, and the most astute. The Hunter label linked to the prestigious Sheldon Hotels would be a certain success. She wondered why she hadn't thought about that the minute she'd heard he had bought the business. She realised with a jolt that she had been too preoccupied with trying to pin underhand motives on him.

She felt uncomfortable as she met his eyes again. 'It's ingenious,' she answered candidly, then, aware of the taunting smile on his lips, added, 'But I'm not sure Paris is the right place to start.'

'It's the right place without question.' He waved away her doubts with complete self-assurance. 'I agree that it won't be the easiest location, but it's the most sensible for us. It will be within easy commuting distance with London, a factor which will be very important to us until we've set up workshops and office premises overseas.' He leaned nonchalantly in his chair, but his dark eyes never left her face. 'Also, it's the romantic capital of the world, and perfect to show Amanda's new collection for the opening fashion show.'

Amanda could hardly take in what he was saying. She knew that her collection was one of the best things she had ever done, but she had never dreamed that it would be shown in Paris! That was something that every struggling young designer yearned for.

'You're going to feature my designs in a Paris show?' She had to ask in case she had misheard.

'Yours will be the only designs used; it will be an exclusive Amanda Hunter presentation,' Drew said calmly.

She was too stunned by the news to say anything for a moment. This was a dream and ambition she had held for a long time; she remembered she had confided this to Drew once while they were engaged. He had laughed and teased her that it was she who was completely wrapped up in her work. Then he had run his hands through her hair and said in a tender voice, 'Hold on to your dream, Amanda. Maybe one day it will come true.'

She wondered if he remembered that evocative moment. Probably not, she thought with a raw ache in her heart as Drew turned to listen as Jordan spoke.

'This will mean we'll have to change a few clauses in Amanda's contract,' the woman had put in.

'We'll see.' Drew frowned and looked over at Amanda, but she didn't meet his eyes; she was looking down at the papers in front of her as if they were all-important. Jordan's use of the word 'we' hadn't escaped her. The two of them were in this together, it seemed, and all they were interested in was profits. She need not have worried about Drew's motives when he took over Hunter's, it had just been a shrewd business move on his part. That knowledge should have comforted her, yet for some strange reason it didn't.

It was a relief when the meeting came to a close. Her thoughts were far too confused for her to be able to concentrate properly on what was being said. She was collecting up her papers when Drew's voice broke into her reverie. 'I would like to talk with you, Amanda, if you wouldn't mind waiting behind.'

Amanda wondered if she had any choice in the matter as she watched the others file out of the room. Only Jordan lingered. She smiled up at Drew. 'Before I begin work there are one or two points I'd like to discuss with you.'

'Yes, I know, Jordan, but it will have to wait until later.' Drew raked a hand through his dark hair. 'Make a start without me and I'll be in as soon as I'm finished here.'

Jordan nodded, but her blue eyes were anything but pleased as she darted a swift look in Amanda's direction on her way out. She was wearing a heavy, cloying perfume which lingered in the air even when the door had closed behind her.

'Miss Lee seems to be quite the little treasure,' Amanda couldn't keep herself from remarking. 'Accountant, adviser—everything rolled into one curvaceous body.'

'She's good at her job,' Drew said coolly.

'She must be good at something,' Amanda muttered with more than a hint of acridity, then, seeing his eyebrows rise, added quickly, 'Well, she's been around for a while, hasn't she?' 'Around' being the operative word, she thought with unusual malice.

'I've employed her for a few years now, yes.' He leaned back in his chair and studied her thoughtfully for a moment. 'I didn't know you'd met her before.'

'Oh, yes, we've met.' She looked towards him directly, unaware of the defiant tilt of her head which exposed the vulnerable, perfect column of her throat. Had Jordan not bothered to inform him of her visit that

morning? she wondered. Probably not, she thought
wryly. Discussing Drew's fiancée would have been at the
very bottom of Jordan's list of priorities.

Drew was watching her intently, probably comparing
her pallor and lacklustre eyes with Jordan's glittering
beauty, she thought darkly. 'Well, Amanda?' he said
suddenly, 'Do I take it from your presence here this
morning that you won't be breaking your contract?'
Although the question was casually asked, his eyes
seemed to burn through her, demanding that she concede
to him.

'Did I have an option?' she asked sharply.

'No, but I'm glad you've decided to be sensible.' His
lips curved derisively. 'Have you brought your designs
in with you?'

She nodded and picked up her leather briefcase from
the side of her chair. Suddenly she didn't want to show
him her work. It wasn't that she had any doubts about
their merit, it was—what was it? Her mind faltered.
Surely it wasn't because of that dress? No! she rejected
that idea violently, yet subversively the thought kept
coming into her mind that the dress had been for his
eyes on their wedding day.

'Well, you'll have to bring them up to me, Amanda.'
His voice held a note of patient amusement. 'I haven't
got X-ray eyes.'

She glared at him before scraping her chair back and
walking towards the head of the table. His eyes wandered over her as she moved, in a cool, leisurely ex-
amination which made her doubt his last statement. That
look made her pulse quicken and warmth suffuse her
cheeks. 'Well, do I pass?' she snapped, irritated with
herself as well as him.

'Very sexy,' he responded, not pretending to mis-
understand. 'I can't help wondering what was going
through your mind when you selected that librarian outfit
this morning.'

'Well, it wasn't sex, that's for sure,' she retorted drily.

'No?' His lips twitched with laughter.

'No,' she said firmly, exasperated at the direction the conversation was taking and the way he was making fun of her. 'Do you want to look at my designs or not?' She flung her case on to the table in front of him.

'Patience, darling, patience,' he censured gently.

The casual use of the endearment was enough to send Amanda's blood-pressure through the ceiling. 'Don't patronise me, and don't call me darling,' she told him stiffly, holding her temper by a mere whisper.

'I don't think you should speak to your boss like that, Amanda. You could hurt his feelings.' He slanted a look at her which was filled with mockery.

'I don't think that's likely, considering my boss is a callous, unfeeling hunk of granite.' It was easy giving full vent to her anger while she was standing over him, but when he stood up, and all six-foot-two of him towered above her, she came to an abrupt halt.

'That's a very provocative statement, Amanda. Would you like me to prove otherwise?' he asked softly.

'I—I—no!' She stumbled away from him, suddenly made afraid by that light in his eyes. 'Keep away from me,' she warned him breathlessly, as he moved closer. 'If you lay one finger on me I'll scream so loud that the whole office block will come running in here! I'll—I'll ruin your reputation,' she finished desperately.

Drew watched her through cool eyes, his mouth twisted in sardonic mockery. 'An impossible task, as it seems to be already ruined.'

'Yes, I suppose seduction in the boardroom would be nothing unusual where you're concerned.' Her skin was flushed, her eyes overbright as she glared at him. 'Only you've got the wrong woman. I'm not interested in you, either in this room or the bedroom.'

'Which room did you have in mind?' he asked in all apparent seriousness, but the glint in his eyes betrayed the fact that he was having fun at her expense, and she itched to slap that contemptuous look off his face.

'Why don't you go and try your arrogant caveman tactics on Miss Lee? I'm sure——' She let out a small cry as Drew suddenly reached for her, hauling her roughly against him.

The contact of her body pressed so closely against his was electrifying. It sent an effusion of fervent emotions flowing through her body. She felt excitement and weakness, mixed with a sensation that was purely desire. She leaned her head against the silk of his shirt, feeling the hard muscles of his chest, breathing in the masculine, tangy scent of his aftershave. A memory flooded her mind, a recollection of them lying naked together, their bodies entwined, feeling, touching, loving.

'Amanda?' His deep voice shattered the silence. She looked up at him, her eyes wide and shadowed with confusion. For a moment their faces were very close. She could see the warm, velvet-brown flecks of colour in his intense, deep gaze, the firm smoothness of his bronzed skin, the sensual curve of his lips. All her senses seemed to cry out for him in that instant, and when he bent his head and his lips took possession of hers the sensation was devastating.

His kiss was gentle at first, exploring the soft curves of her lips, then hungrily it plundered with a fierce demand which fired warning signals to her brain. She was too aroused to pay them any heed, her arms stealing upwards so that her fingers could twine themselves through his thick, dark hair. Her body was pressing closer, driven by an insatiable need to be next to his very skin.

His hands were unfastening the top buttons of her suit. She could feel his touch against the soft bareness of her throat. Then his lips left hers to trail a line of fire down its creamy, sensitive column.

'Oh, God, Amanda...I want you.' The low, rasping words brought cold reality hurtling back into her body.

'No!' Suddenly she was tearing herself away from him, her breath catching in painful gasps. The kind of wanting he was talking about had no tender emotions attached to it. He didn't care about her, he had made that perfectly clear long ago.

'That isn't what your body and your lips were telling me a few moments ago.' His eyes were dark, inscrutable, the strong planes of his face tense.

'Maybe I just felt like turning the tables on you, manipulating you just the way you are me,' she jeered with a dispassion she was far from feeling.

She was unprepared for the storm of anger her words seemed to rouse in him. His whole face clouded with it, so that he loomed over her, powerful and very threatening.

'Someone should have warned you about playing with fire.' The words were calmly spoken, but that steely control he was exercising only served to frighten her more. He stretched out a hand and caught the top of her arm in a vicelike grip which burned through the thin material of her suit. 'And I'm going to show you what happens to teasing, tormenting little vixens.'

She stared at him, weak, breathless, her full lips slightly apart. She was afraid, yet when he lowered his dark head and crushed his lips against hers, her heart constricted. This time his kiss was brutal, punishing. It ground against the softness of her mouth, demanding and hard. She gave a faint groan under the fierceness of that caress, needing him, wanting him. The external pain he was inflicting was nothing to the pain she felt deep inside.

'Drew, please,' she murmured brokenly. He hesitated, his breath warm over her lips. Then abruptly he moved back from her, swearing inaudibly under his breath.

'Did that make you feel good?' Her voice wavered precariously, and her emerald-green eyes shone with unshed tears.

'Amanda——' His voice was gentle, concerned. He reached to touch the arm he had held so roughly, and she flinched away. If he said something kind and compassionate now, she would break down. That he might guess how deeply that kiss had affected her would be the last straw; she would die from the humiliation.

'Don't say anything, Drew,' she said quickly, unsteadily. 'I guess the loathing I feel towards you is mutual. There's no point making things worse.'

The door opened beside them and Jordan walked in. 'Drew?' The brightness of her tone belied the narrowed blue eyes which took in the closeness of their stance, the silken strands of hair which had escaped from the clips in Amanda's hair.

Amanda turned her back on the other woman, touching her bruised lips with self-conscious fingers.

'Yes, what is it, Jordan?' The clipped anger in Drew's voice flayed Amanda's raw nerves; she knew that anger was really directed at her.

'I'm sorry if I'm interrupting.' Jordan sounded anything but sorry. 'But I can't start on any work until I've talked to you.'

'Yes, all right, I'm coming now.' Drew sounded suddenly weary. 'Your designs are on the table, Amanda,' he told her brusquely, before the door closed behind them.

Amanda found herself shivering, her emotions at fever-pitch. She had made a complete fool of herself. Why had she let him touch her like that? Why had she responded so passionately to him? She didn't dare dwell on the way she had lost control so easily.

With trembling hands she secured the stray wisps of hair back into the severe topknot and buttoned the top of her suit. What made it all so much worse was the fact that Jordan had witnessed how foolish she had looked. Angry with herself, she picked up her briefcase from the table and headed towards her office.

She heard the sound of Jordan's husky laughter even before she turned the corner and saw them both in her office! Jordan was seated at Amanda's desk, looking adoringly up at Drew who stood beside her, his arm lightly resting on her shoulder. They looked close, intimate, and it made Amanda's stomach clench into knots. She wondered what they were talking about and what Jordan was finding so amusing. She stepped forward, exasperated with herself for caring.

'Ah, here's your designer now.' Jordan's words made her wonder if it had been her they had been discussing with such humour. The thought made her eyes glimmer like ice-cold jade as she met Drew's impenetrable dark gaze.

'I forgot to tell you that I've given your office to Jordan,' he stated calmly. 'I've moved your things into the main office. We can share for the time being.'

Amanda's delicate eyebrows rose. Share an office with him? She couldn't think of anything more disturbing, and how dared he give her office to Jordan without even so much as mentioning it to her? 'Really?' Her voice was cold and her eyes flicked over both of them with equal disdain. 'Well, that's all right, I'll just pack everything up again. I'd prefer to work at home, anyway.' With that she turned her back and walked stiffly from the room.

'Amanda.' She hadn't taken more than two steps when Drew's voice called her back. She turned and saw him striding towards her. She could almost feel his anger, lying just beneath the surface, like a cold, impenetrable barrier between them. 'You will leave your things exactly where they are,' he demanded in a low, furious voice.

'I don't want to work in the same office as you,' she answered stubbornly.

'Tough.' His dark eyes seemed to gouge straight through her. 'And, while we're on the subject, I want all your work done in the office from now on.'

Amanda stared at him, horrified; there would be no chance of her getting anything done if he was around watching her every move. 'I've always done most of my work at home. Why do you want me to change now?'

'Because I say so, that's why.' He watched her impatiently. 'These designs are going to be top priority for the next few months and I don't want any Tom, Dick or Harry waltzing into your house and taking a look at them.'

'I've never shown my designs to anyone,' she stormed furiously.

'No—not even your boyfriend?' One eyebrow lifted sardonically.

'I'm very professional about my work and I never show my designs to anyone outside these offices,' she reiterated.

'I'm very glad to hear it,' he drawled. 'Now you can be even more professional *in* your office, where you won't have any interruptions.'

'I don't have any interruptions at home.'

'James doesn't bring a bottle of wine around every day, then?' he asked scornfully.

'He did that on my day off, and what I do in my spare time is my business.'

'And what you do during working hours is mine,' he told her firmly. 'So get yourself into that office and start doing something.' With that he turned and headed back towards what was now Jordan's office. 'Oh, and Amanda,' he paused with his hand on the door-handle, 'if you're worried that I might disturb you—then don't, because I'll be spending as little time as I possibly can in an office with you.'

'Good,' she said coolly and turned away, surprised to find that, for some strange reason, that last gibe had really hurt.

He opened the door and she could hear Jordan's voice clearly. 'Drew, about this evening, could we make it eight o'clock, only——'

'Yes, eight will be fine,' Drew cut in heavily. The door closed and the rest of the conversation was lost to Amanda. She headed angrily towards his office. What sort of man kissed you almost senseless and then a little while later made a date with his girlfriend? she wondered grimly.

Amanda was tired when she got home that evening. Tired and in a very black mood. The sight of James's Porsche parked outside her house made her sigh heavily. He got out of the car as her taxi pulled up, and stood waiting for her.

He was wearing a long, dark overcoat, and he wrapped it closer around him and put his hands in the deep pockets. It was a bitterly cold March day, and she could see his breath misting in the sharp air.

'Hello, honey.' He smiled as she stepped out of the taxi. 'You're late home, aren't you?'

Her eyebrows rose in surprise. Since when had James started to keep tabs on her? she wondered. And why was he waiting outside her house at this hour? 'I've had a hectic day at the office.' She put her key in the latch and the door swung open into a pleasantly warm hall.

'Thank God for central heating,' James remarked appreciatively as he followed her in and slung the heavy coat he had been wearing over the nearest chair.

'Haven't you been working today?' Amanda asked, noticing the smart grey suit he was wearing. Usually James dressed casually for work in jeans and a sweater.

'Yes, but I finished early and I thought you might like to go out to dinner.'

Amanda wrinkled her nose. 'I'm sorry, James, but I'm so tired. All I want to do is have a shower and an early night.'

'Perhaps tomorrow night, then?' He looked disappointed.

She nodded and then suddenly remembered—'Oh, no, I can't tomorrow. My father is throwing that party for Drew tomorrow and he'll be expecting me to attend.'

'So you're still going through with that charade?' he asked flatly.

She nodded and moved into the kitchen to put the kettle on. 'Would you like a coffee?'

'Please.' He watched her from the doorway for a while, a curious expression on his face. 'How was your day at Sheldon Enterprises?'

She smiled wryly at him. 'I think the name of the place is the only thing he *hasn't* changed.'

'What other changes is he making, then?' James moved into the room and sat down at the kitchen table.

'Well, for a start, he doesn't want me working at home any more, and he's kicked me out of my office and into his,' she told him calmly, as she poured coffee into two china beakers. 'As you can guess, I've had a wonderful day,' she added sarcastically.

'That man's got a bloody nerve!' James's blue eyes clouded furiously. 'I hope you told him what to do with his job.'

'I would have loved to, but unfortunately I'm not in any position to do that, am I?'

'You mean you're simply going to put up with it?' He jumped up from his seat, ignoring the drink that she had put in front of him. 'My God, Amanda, you know what his next move will be, don't you?' He glared at her.

'No, but I've got a feeling you're going to tell me.' She sat down, her head throbbing with a tense headache. She could have done without this after the day she had just had.

'It's obvious.' He glowered at her. 'He's going to make a pass at you.'

She could feel heat flowing into her face as she thought about the way Drew had kissed her this morning. James's eyes narrowed suspiciously on her. 'That is, unless he already has?'

'Drew isn't interested in me,' she prevaricated. 'Besides, he already has his very attractive girlfriend installed at the office.' She glanced at her watch. It was just after seven, and Drew would probably be getting ready for his date with Jordan. She wondered where they would go. Out for dinner, maybe, and then what? Back to his place? Her head throbbed painfully.

'You're forgetting that, for Drew Sheldon, variety is the spice of life,' muttered James. 'It will be a matter of pride to him if he's able to get you back from me, if only so that he can dump you when it suits him.'

'I'm not forgetting anything,' Amanda answered bleakly. 'But it has nothing to do with you, James. There's nothing between us, remember? We're just good friends.'

'That's not strictly true, on my part, anyway.' He moved over towards her and crouched down so that his face was on a level with hers. For a moment she couldn't help comparing that blond, pallid countenance with Drew's vital, powerful darkness.

'Amanda, do you remember that evening when you and Drew split? That evening when he came around here and found us together?'

Amanda closed her eyes; she didn't want to remember that nightmare time.

'Amanda?' He shook her slightly. 'You were on the point of giving yourself to me that night. If Drew hadn't arrived, you and I would——'

'No!' Her eyes flew open, vivid and emphatic. 'No, James, nothing would have happened. I was upset and I wasn't thinking clearly, but——'

'There are some things that you shouldn't think too deeply about,' he interrupted. 'You should just feel.' Before she realised his intentions, his lips were against hers, eager and demanding.

For a moment she was stunned, her lips unresponsive against the fire of his. The thought flashed through her mind that this was the second time today that a man had kissed her without her consent. Only this kiss did nothing to ignite her senses, she felt no answering need springing to life inside her.

'Stop it, James!' She tried to push him away, but his lips became more intent, filled with an avidity that left her cold. 'Please!' She desperately tried to break free, but he didn't seem to notice her distress. She struck out at him angrily, catching him on the side of his face with a stinging slap.

Immediately he released her and moved back, raking a hand through his dishevelled fair hair. For a moment his eyes looked bright and resentful, then suddenly they clouded with anxiety, as they took in how distraught she was. 'God, Amanda, I'm sorry.' His voice held a slight tremor. She wanted to tell him it was all right, but to her horror she could feel tears welling up inside her.

'Just go,' she managed to whisper throatily. He hesitated for only a minute, then he was gone. As she heard the door close behind him, Amanda buried her head in her arms and wept.

CHAPTER FIVE

IT WASN'T just James's behaviour that had upset her so forcibly; normally she would have been able to cope with a situation like that calmly.

Amanda sat up and tried to pull herself together. It had been the culmination of a day fraught with emotional tension. Just being in the same room as Drew had disturbed her more than she cared to admit, even to herself. And when he had kissed her—she closed her eyes and took a deep, shaky breath—she didn't dare contemplate the tumultuous feelings that had generated. Now Drew would be out somewhere with Jordan, and one thing was certain—he wouldn't be wasting any time thinking about her.

James was right about one fact, Drew did still have the power to hurt her. Poor James, she had handled that delicate situation this evening very badly. But he had taken her completely by surprise, for he had never made any advances towards her like that before. He had placed an arm around her occasionally, kissed her on the cheek once or twice, but it had only been in a brotherly fashion. At least, that was how she had regarded it; she had thought she had made her feelings towards him clear long ago. Guiltily she wondered if somehow she had misled him into thinking differently. He had mentioned that evening, the one just after she had discovered Jordan in Drew's hotel suite. Even though it was an episode that had occurred over a year ago, the memory was still vivid, the pain still sharp.

She got up from her chair and poured the two cups of cold coffee down the sink. Then she turned towards the refrigerator and took out a chilled bottle of wine. She would have a glass of wine, some bread and cheese and watch something on TV, anything to distract her troubled thoughts.

It was strange how something as simple as switching on a light switch could conjure up a memory so vivid. Amanda sat down in her living-room and pressed a trembling hand to her forehead. For a split second she had almost been able to see Drew staring at her as he had on that night long ago, in this very room...

She had been out with James to the theatre. Her mouth twisted ruefully; she couldn't even remember what they had been to see. Her tortured mind had been filled with pictures of Drew and Jordan together. She had relived every word Jordan had said to her that morning at his hotel suite.

When they had got back to her dark house late that night, her control had snapped, her brave face had vanished along with the crowds they had been among. She hadn't put the lights on in the living-room; she didn't want James to see the anguish on her face as she went into his arms.

'God, I've dreamed of this moment,' he had breathed into her hair. 'You're so beautiful!'

'Oh, James...' She had been going to tell him it was Drew she wanted to cling to, Drew she loved, but she never got the chance. A low, throbbing voice in the corner of the room had interrupted her words and sent her spinning around in shock.

'Yes, very desirable, but you'll have to put a ring on her finger if you want to go to bed with her.'

Light had flooded the room as James dived to switch it on with a trembling hand.

'At least, that was the impression I got.' Drew had been sitting in one of the chairs by the window, his manner relaxed, a glass of whisky in one hand. Only his eyes were out of control, wild and dark with furious rage. 'I see I needn't have worried about you feeling lonely while I'm away. You seem to be occupying yourself very well.'

'How the hell did you get in here?' James had run a hand through his thick blond hair, leaving it unruly.

'My darling fiancée gave me a key.' Drew had stared directly into Amanda's eyes. 'I presume it slipped your mind that I arrived back today?'

'No.' She'd licked her lips nervously. By the harsh note in his voice she had known he was holding his temper with steel-like restraint. She had wanted to scream accusations at him, tell him she knew all about his sordid affair. But pride had stood in her way. Let him think that *she* was having an affair, let him feel humiliated the way she had that very morning. In that instant she had wanted revenge.

'Look here, Sheldon, I think you should leave. Amanda doesn't want you here.'

'Amanda has always been capable of speaking for herself in the past.' Drew had stood up slowly from his chair and she had trembled at the menacing power of his frame as he walked towards her. 'Well, Amanda, do you want me here or not?'

She had swallowed convulsively, her eyes locked on his compelling features. Every bone in her body had longed to go into his arms; she had wanted him even then.

As he'd reached forceful arms out to hold her shoulders, James had made the mistake of catching his arm. 'She doesn't want you, Sheldon. She said as much tonight.'

It was then that Drew had hit him. With one sure, powerful blow he had knocked him clear across the room. Amanda had stifled a cry of distress as she moved to help him up, but Drew held her firmly with an iron grip, his hands bruising her through the thin material of her blouse.

'How long have you been seeing him behind my back?' he had demanded roughly. 'How long?'

'I—I haven't. Stop it, Drew, stop it!' Her eyes had misted with tears; she couldn't bear the way he was talking to her, the way he was looking at her.

'Oh, don't turn on the innocent little girl act, I fell for that once before. I'm not stupid enough to do it again.'

She had struggled to get free of him, her breath catching with sobs. 'Get away from me, Drew, just get away!'

He had let go of her abruptly and she had stumbled back from him. She had never seen him look so angry; he was scrutinising her as if he was seeing her for the first time. There had been contempt in his deep eyes, his mouth drawn in a tight line. That look had brought all her anger surging to her rescue.

'Now get out of here,' she had ordered.

The dark eyes became insolent in their regard. 'Don't worry, I'm going. I'm not interested in second-hand goods.'

She had gasped with pain and shock at his cutting words. Wrenching the large emerald engagement ring off her finger, she had pushed it at him.

'Are you sleeping with him?' The question had been wrung from his lips, his large hands trapping her delicate ones. The ring had stabbed into the softness of her skin, yet the pain had been lost among the much greater one of losing him.

'There's more to love than sex, Drew, but I suppose you wouldn't know the difference, you've had so many affairs.' She had spoken calmly, her anger giving her back her self-respect.

He had made no reply, just stared at her as if he would have liked to crush the life out of her body.

That was the way she remembered him now, staring at her with contempt. That look was probably a million light years away from the way he would be looking at Jordan this evening. Her head pounded unmercifully. Leaving her food and wine untouched, she went upstairs to search for some pain-killers. Then she decided to have an early night.

'You look like death warmed up,' Drew remarked drily the moment Amanda walked into the office the next morning.

'But your kind words make me feel so much better,' she said with sarcasm. Taking her seat at her desk, she pulled the dust-sheet off her work, and glared at the paper in front of her. She had hardly managed to do any work yesterday.

'What's the matter?' Drew grinned at her. 'Having boyfriend problems?'

'Is your private life really so boring that you have to pry into mine?' she asked caustically.

He laughed, unperturbed. 'Let me guess—James is demanding you give your job up.'

She frowned, irritated by his perception. 'On the contrary, we had a quiet, romantic evening,' she found herself lying, and gained a good deal of satisfaction when she saw the smile fade from his face.

'Your idyllic evening doesn't seem to have left you starry-eyed,' he observed, and pushed the button on his intercom. 'Sandy, bring us in some coffee, will you?'

'I could say the same about you; you're not exactly full of the joys of spring.' She glanced over at him; she might be able to comment on his mood but never his looks. It was unfair that the man was so damn handsome. 'Let me guess—there aren't enough days in the week to keep all your women happy,' she quipped with a sharp edge in her voice.

'Time is one of many problems.' His dark eyes gleamed with lazy amusement. 'But I'm pleased to say that keeping women happy has never been one of them.'

'Except for me, of course,' she couldn't resist saying. 'There's always an exception to the rule.'

The amusement evaporated from his eyes and it was hard to tell what was going on behind their cool, dark scrutiny.

Amanda was relieved when the door opened, breaking the chilly silence. Sandy came in carrying an enormous bouquet of red roses.

'These have just arrived for you, Miss Hunter,' she said, smiling broadly and putting them down on Amanda's desk.

'They're beautiful!' exclaimed Amanda in delighted surprise. She bent and breathed in their sweet aroma, wondering who could have sent them. There was a card attached and she opened it. 'Please forgive me,' was written in James's embellished handwriting, and then his name underlined with a sweep of his pen.

She looked up as Sandy disappeared out of the room to get some water for them. 'They're from James,' she said softly, almost to herself.

'Must have been one hell of an argument,' Drew said drily. 'I think old James is worried.'

She glared at him. 'No—just romantic.'

'Well, at least he's succeeded in bringing a sparkle back into your eyes.' His lips curved in a mocking smile, before he turned his attention to opening his morning mail.

Sandy came back in with a tray of coffee and a vase for the flowers. 'Would you like me to arrange them for you, Miss Hunter?' she offered helpfully.

Amanda nodded. 'Thank you, Sandy.' She wondered if she should ring James and thank him. It had been a lovely gesture for him to send her flowers, but she couldn't help but speculate whether he had done it entirely for her benefit. Had he sent roses to the office so that Drew would notice them? He had never done anything like this before, but then he had never kissed her the way he had done last night. Perhaps he was genuinely just apologising.

She glanced over at Drew. From the stern look on his face she decided to wait until later to phone James, then she would be able to speak to him privately.

'Good morning.' Jordan walked into the office, a wide smile on her face. She looked radiantly beautiful in a pink suit, which was tailored cleverly to appear businesslike and yet sexy at the same time. 'I've brought the first half of those figures you wanted, Drew.'

'Ah, wonderful!' Drew cast his eye quickly over the papers she handed him. 'You get more efficient by the day, if that's possible.'

'Flattery will get you everywhere,' she said teasingly, a pleased smile on her ruby-red lips. 'Actually, I surprised even myself at the speed I was able to prepare them. We were so late last night——' Her voice trailed off evocatively as she turned and looked at Amanda. 'Oh, good morning, Amanda, I didn't see you there behind the door.'

Amanda smiled and tried not to roll her eyes. The woman would have had to be blind not to notice her, and she made it sound as if she were stuck in a cubbyhole instead of the most luxurious office.

Her eye caught the roses on Amanda's desk. 'What beautiful flowers! Is there a special occasion I should know about?'

'No,' Amanda answered bluntly, and then, aware that she had sounded churlish, tacked on, 'No occasion.'

'Oh, come now, Amanda.' Drew's eyes met hers mockingly across the room. 'Of course there's something to celebrate. A romantic impulse and starting work for your new boss; there are two reasons to start with.'

Amanda wanted to tell him to get lost, but she managed to smile coolly at him. 'If you say so.'

'How sweet.' Jordan's voice was light, but her eyes were chilly as they contemplated Amanda.

Did she imagine that the flowers were from Drew? Amanda wondered. Suddenly she couldn't help feeling a little sorry for the other woman; it seemed even she wasn't totally sure of Drew. Amanda knew that feeling only too well. She was about to clarify the fact that it hadn't been Drew who had sent the bouquet, when the buzzer on Drew's desk interrupted her.

'Ah, I shall have to leave you, ladies.' Drew stood up from his desk. 'I'm interviewing some applicants in the boardroom today for the position of manager.'

Amanda's eyebrows rose. 'A manager for Hunter's?'

'Yes, don't look so surprised. I won't have the time to come into the offices every day. I'm going to need someone taking control of things from this end.'

'Of course.' Amanda looked down at her work. It made sense that a busy man like Drew would hand over the reins of this small business to someone else. Yet she found herself remembering his words yesterday. 'I'll be spending as little time as I possibly can in an office with you.'

'Have you brought your finished designs in with you, Amanda?'

Drew's question brought her out of her reverie. 'Yes.' She tapped the portfolio beside her.

'Good. I'll just place them in the safe until I have time to look at them.' Drew picked them up. 'If I don't get a chance to speak to you today, I'll see you this evening at your father's house.'

'I suppose so,' Amanda answered indifferently.

'Would you like me to pick you up? You're on my way.'

'No, thanks,' she said quickly. She was dreading the thought of this party, anyway. The idea of travelling to it in the same car with Jordan and him made her nerves quiver alarmingly.

'Please yourself.' He shrugged carelessly. 'I'll see you later, Jordan.'

Jordan nodded, but made no move to leave the room.

When the door closed behind Drew, Amanda reached for the coffee-pot that Sandy had left on her desk, and poured herself a cup. Good manners prompted her to look over to where Jordan was still lounging against Drew's desk. 'Coffee?'

'Black, no sugar.' Jordan watched as she poured her a cup and then sauntered over to pick it up. 'I'm so looking forward to this evening, I just love parties,' she said, glancing around and then sitting in one of the large, comfortable armchairs. 'Of course, Drew and I attend so many that it can be a bit of a headache sometimes. Well, you know how it is, trying to decide on a new dress for each occasion.' She sipped her coffee, and her blue eyes had a derisory light in them. 'That's why I was so pleased when Drew bought Hunter Fashions; now I'll have an endless selection of clothes at my fingertips. Drew does like to spoil me, you know.'

'Really?' Amanda managed to inject a bored note into her voice. The thought of Drew dishing out her designs to Jordan Lee made her blood boil. She wondered if that was the purpose behind this seemingly ingenuous conversation. 'Well, Drew always was generous.'

'Yes, I'd forgotten you were once engaged.' The sneer in the woman's voice told her very clearly that Jordan had forgotten nothing. That morning outside Drew's hotel suite was probably as clear in Jordan's memory as it was in her own. 'Of course, one must be civilised about these things, but I still think you're very plucky to be able to continue working for Drew under the circumstances.'

'And what circumstances are those?' asked Amanda, meeting the woman's steel-blue eyes.

'Well, I simply meant that if a man had jilted me as Drew did you, I don't think I would be able to work for him.'

'I don't think I would, either,' Amanda said calmly. 'But as Drew didn't jilt me, I have no problems.'

Jordan's finely arched eyebrows rose. 'Oh, dear, I should never have mentioned that, it was very indelicate of me.' She gave an embarrassed little laugh which rang very false.

'On the contrary, I'm glad you did, so that I could correct your misconceptions,' Amanda answered sweetly. 'Is there anything else you'd like to know before I get back to work?'

'No, I don't think so.' Jordan finished her coffee and put the cup down on Amanda's desk. 'After all, your affair with Drew is very much in the past and forgotten.' She got to her feet and then hesitated. 'Oh, there was something else. Drew tells me you're working on a simply stunning collection for wedding dresses.'

'I'm trying to, yes,' Amanda said quietly.

'Well, I was wondering if I could look through them some time; you see, I'll be needing a wedding dress in the near future.'

'I didn't know you were engaged.' Amanda took a sip of coffee and stared at Jordan over the rim of her cup.

'It's very hush-hush at the moment. Drew doesn't want the staff to know about it. He thinks it will put a strain on our working relationship,' said Jordan with a glinting little smile.

Amanda couldn't begin to analyse the emotions that raced through her at that piece of information. There was a cold feeling in the pit of her stomach—shock, she supposed. Even though she had known about Drew's affair with this woman, she had never thought it was serious. She had come to terms with the fact that Drew was a womaniser long ago. He was a sensualist who liked variety; he enjoyed the chase more than the kill. Was he really going to change all that for Jordan?

'Congratulations.' She managed to smile at the woman, but inside she felt numb, dead. 'But I'm afraid you won't be able to look at my designs until they're shown at my fashion show.'

'Oh, dear!' Jordan wrinkled her nose. 'Well, never mind. I can wait, it won't be that long.' She moved to the door. 'Don't mention any of this to Drew, will you, Amanda? He might not want you to know.'

'No, he might not,' Amanda muttered.

* * *

'Hello, Amanda. Am I forgiven?' James's voice sounded unusually tentative at the other end of the phone.

'Yes, of course, let's just forget it.' Amanda slipped off her shoes and curled up on her settee. 'I meant to ring you earlier, but I've been so busy at the office today.'

'How are things going?'

'All right.' She bit her lip. Things were anything but all right. The only good thing about her day was the fact that she hadn't set eyes on Drew since he had stepped out of his office this morning. 'Thank you for the roses, they were beautiful.'

'I'm glad you liked them. Look, Amanda, I'm really sorry about the way I acted yesterday. I was insensitive and completely out of...'

'It doesn't matter, James,' she cut in quickly.

'Then are we still on for the party tonight?' There was that strained, hesitant note in his voice again.

Amanda didn't know what to say. She would have liked James to accompany her for moral support. But she was frightened he would read something into it. Yesterday had made her realise how blind she had been where James was concerned. She didn't want to lead him on or give him any false hopes.

'Please, Amanda, I would really like to escort you,' James prompted into the heavy silence, then added quickly, 'We are still friends, aren't we?'

'Yes, of course.' Amanda weakened; after all, it was only a party. They had attended enough of them in the past; one more wasn't going to make any difference. 'Well, if you're sure?'

'Certain. What time shall I pick you up?' he asked swiftly.

'It starts at eight.'

'Fine. I'll be round at seven-thirty.' The phone went dead, almost as if he was frightened she would change her mind if he delayed. She replaced the receiver thoughtfully. He was probably right. She didn't want to go to the party in the first place.

She felt a little better after she had soaked in a perfumed bath and washed her hair. She gazed at her naked
body as she dried it with a large, fluffy towel. No man
had ever touched her apart from Drew; he was the only
man she had ever wanted. The recollection of his lips
against hers rose unbidden in her mind. She shivered,
her body aching with sudden deep yearning. Immediately she felt impatient with herself. Drew was a closed
episode in her life and he was about to marry Jordan
Lee. She wondered how she would feel when she watched
them together this evening, knowing they were in love,
knowing that Jordan was the woman Drew had decided
to spend the rest of his life with.

She lingered over choosing what to wear, finally deciding on a silk dress in a glorious shade of emerald. It
was a sophisticated dress with a round halter-neck, richly
encrusted with crystals, and a deep, plunging back which
meant she could wear little underneath it.

She applied a little mascara to her dark eyelashes and
some coral lipstick. She needed no other make-up; her
skin was luminous and faintly flushed, her hair lending
soft warmth to it as it fell loose in soft, shining waves
around her shoulders.

She glanced at her watch. James would be here any
minute. Quickly she sprayed her favourite Opium
perfume around her neck and wrists, and picked up her
clutch-bag and silk stole. With a last look in the mirror
she went downstairs to wait. It was very silly, but it
seemed extra-important that she should look her best
tonight. She tried to tell herself that she needed the confidence looking good would give her, but deep down she
knew that wasn't the only reason.

James whistled with appreciation as he caught sight
of her. 'You look fantastic!'

'Thank you, kind sir,' she laughed, and stood back
from the door so that he could come in. 'Would you
like a drink before we go?' She knew she was only trying
to delay the moment of leaving. She felt nervous, which

was ridiculous; she was going to a party at her father's house, not to the dentist. What was it that was bothering her? she wondered. The thought that Drew was going to be there? She was going to have to get used to that.

James nodded. 'Yes, I'll have a Scotch, please.' He watched as she turned to pour his drink. The dress she wore moulded to her slender curves, accentuating her tiny waist. 'Amanda, about last night,' he began hesitantly.

She turned and looked at him through reserved eyes. 'I thought we agreed to forget about that.'

'Yes.' He took the drink she held out to him and his hand brushed against hers. 'But we need to talk.'

'Maybe,' she agreed gently. 'But not tonight. I've got a lot on my mind, what with work and Drew...'

'He came to see me at my studio today,' James cut in.

'Drew did?' Amanda's eyebrows rose. 'What did he want?'

'He asked if I intended picking up my work option with Hunter's at the end of the month.'

'Oh...and do you?' Amanda asked curiously.

James shrugged. 'I don't see why not. If you're able to work for him, then there's no reason why I shouldn't.'

'I quite agree.' Amanda turned and poured herself a glass of Perrier water. 'So you told him yes?'

'I did. Then he promptly offered me an assignment in Bermuda, photographing one of his hotels for a brochure.'

'He did?' Amanda whirled around, her eyes alive with excitement. 'That's wonderful, James!'

'You think so?' James asked grimly, and tossed back his drink. 'I think he offered it to me hoping he'd lose me in the Bermuda triangle.'

Amanda laughed and shook her head. 'I think you're getting paranoid where Drew's concerned.'

'Maybe so.' James didn't look amused. 'But I still turned the offer down.'

'James, you're crazy! It would have been a fantastic job. Why did you turn it down?'

'Because Drew was trying to separate us and I don't want that. Amanda, I love you, and I want to marry you.'

Amanda ran a troubled hand through her hair. 'Oh, James, I don't know what to say.' She stared at him across the room, a wealth of confusion and sadness in her eyes at his quietly spoken words. She supposed she should have expected this after his display of emotion yesterday, but he had completely taken her by surprise.

'Just say yes, Amanda,' he pleaded quietly. 'I could make you happy, I know I could.'

'James, you're sweet and kind and very dear to me.' Amanda took a steadying breath; she didn't want to hurt him but she had to be truthful. 'I can't marry you, James, because I don't love you.'

His hand tightened around his empty glass so that his knuckles gleamed white. 'Don't say no straight away, Amanda. At least do me the honour of thinking about it.'

She looked away from him. 'I . . . I don't need to think about it, James . . . I know my feelings won't change.'

'I'm not going to give up on you.' He put his glass down on the table, his face set in a grim mask of anger. 'I suppose we'd better leave for this damn party.'

There was a strained silence as James manoeuvred the sleek Porsche among the busy London traffic. Then they were out of the city and into the countryside. Amanda leaned back in her seat and shot an oblique look at the surly expression on James's face.

'I know you're hurt and angry right now,' she said gently. 'But one day you'll meet the right girl and you'll be glad you didn't marry me.'

James changed down gears with a violent clashing, but remained silent.

'You shouldn't have refused Drew's offer, it had nothing to do with trying to separate us,' Amanda continued, desperately trying to make him see sense. 'I mean nothing to Drew, he's in love with someone else.'

'Why are you still carrying a torch for him, then?' James suddenly demanded furiously.

'I'm not,' Amanda denied emphatically.

The Porsche scraped dangerously near the gateposts as James swung it into the driveway of her old home.

'If you say so,' he muttered drily.

Amanda didn't bother to answer him. There was a cold feeling of dread spiralling up inside her, as the car rounded a corner and her father's home came into view.

Fairy-lights were strung along the trees, giving a colourful glow to the darkness. They reflected over the multitude of cars that lined the drive, from sporty models to the gleaming opulence of Rolls-Royces. James pulled up at the front door, and her father's chauffeur came down the steps to park the car for them.

Amanda stepped out into the cold night air, and for a moment she stood looking up at the house. She had spent a lot of happy times here. Her own engagement party with Drew—that had been a magical evening. The old Georgian manor house held a lot of memories for her, both happy and sad.

James slipped a proprietorial arm around her waist, but she didn't protest. Somehow she felt she needed his support as they went up to the front door.

It opened to warmth, laughter and the hum of people enjoying themselves. Chandeliers blazed twinkling lights over the crowds of people milling about in the entrance hall. The doors to both lounges at either side of the hall were open. In one people were dancing to a three-piece orchestra, in the other people sat in the soft settees and chairs or just stood around talking.

A maid who was unfamiliar to Amanda took her wrap from her. Amanda guessed her father had probably hired extra help for the evening.

'I don't know about you, but I could use another drink,' muttered James. He signalled to a passing waiter. Amanda was too busy looking about her to bother about drinking. Unconsciously she was searching for Drew's tall figure among the crowd.

'Hello, Miss Hunter.' Her father's major domo made his way towards them through the crowd. 'It's nice to see you again.'

'Hello, Saunders.' Amanda smiled warmly at the elderly man. 'Have you seen my father anywhere on your travels?'

'Yes, I believe he's in the reception room.' Saunders waved towards the room where music was drifting out. 'If you'll excuse me, Miss Hunter, I have to go and check on the food. You can't trust these catering companies, you know.'

'He's as efficient as ever,' remarked James drily as they moved into the other room. 'He always reminds me of a sergeant-major.'

'Yes, I think he reminds the staff of one as well.' Amanda glanced around, and her heart suddenly stopped beating, the smile slipped from her lips. A few feet away from her, Drew was standing by the dance-floor talking to a group of men. In his formal black evening wear he had a dangerous attraction, the cut of his suit emphasising his athletic, hard-muscled body: the broad sweep of his shoulders, the strong chest and tapering slimness from waist to hips. Her eyes drank in the sight of him as if he were an intoxicating drink.

He turned his head as if suddenly aware of her presence and their eyes locked. The rest of the room seemed to melt away, the noise, the people, everything, as she gazed into the darkness of his eyes.

'Darling.' James's voice close to her ear startled her out of her reverie. She turned, surprised to find his face so near to hers that she could smell the faint trace of alcohol on his breath. 'Your father is over by the french doors, do you want to sit with him?' Amanda nodded and followed him through the room.

She was relieved to see that her father was looking a lot better than he had been a couple of days ago in the office. When she said as much, he laughed. 'Retirement is wonderful, Amanda, wish I'd done it years ago. Now, tell me, how are things at the office?'

'Fine.' Amanda smiled, and took the seat beside him. 'Everything is running very smoothly.'

From where she was sitting she could see Drew clearly. She noticed Jordan making her way towards him. She wore a red, sequined dress which hugged her slim figure and glittered electrifyingly under the coloured lights around the dance-floor. Amanda felt a sharp pain shoot through her as Jordan reached his side and reached up to kiss his cheek.

'Wake up, Amanda.'

She jumped guiltily as James touched her arm. 'Sorry, were you saying something?'

He nodded. 'I asked if you wanted to dance.'

'Yes, all right.' She didn't really want to, but she felt it would be churlish to refuse.

James slipped his arms around her and held her close as they swayed to the rhythm of the music. 'You love him, don't you?' he asked suddenly, his voice soft and gentle against her ear.

She sighed. 'James, my refusal has nothing to do with Drew. Look, why don't you tell him you've changed your mind about that job? I'm sure it won't be too late.'

'You angling to get rid of me now, Amanda?' He pulled away slightly to look into her eyes.

'Don't be silly. I'm just concerned that you've turned down a good opportunity for all the wrong reasons.' To her surprise he bent and kissed her cheek gently. 'Don't look now, honey, but I think that man you can't stand is making his way over towards us.'

Amanda glanced around and her heart seemed to do a somersault as she saw Drew standing beside them. 'Mind if I cut in, Reece?' he asked, but his eyes never left Amanda's face.

CHAPTER SIX

'No, I don't mind. She's all yours, for the time being, anyway.' James's flippant remark belied the coldness in his blue eyes as he stepped back. Amanda shot him a furious look. He made her sound like some sort of parcel he was passing on! She would have walked off the dance-floor and ignored both of them, only Drew arrogantly swept her away before she had time to move.

The music changed to a slower, dreamy melody. She tried to hold herself stiffly away from him as he held her in his strong arms.

'Was I interrupting a romantic moment?' he taunted softly.

She glared up at him, angry at his mocking tone but even more angry at her body's instant response to the pleasure of being held by him. 'Not really, I have my romantic moments in private,' she answered primly.

A hard glitter entered the sardonic coolness of his eyes. 'Well, if you want to keep it that way, you should wear something a little less seductive.' He moved her closer towards him and his hand rested on the bare skin of her back. The light touch made her shiver with desire and her body moved of its own accord to press closer to him.

'You look beautiful tonight, Amanda, so beautiful.' His lips touched her hair softly. The sensation made her tingle, and she couldn't think of anything except being as close to him as possible. Impulsively she wound her arms up and around his neck, twining her fingers through his thick, dark hair.

'Do you remember how we danced like this at our engagement party?' His voice was deep and hypnotic, close to her ear.

'Yes, I remember.' Was that her voice, so husky and breathless? She looked up at him, her eyes wide and brilliant emerald. For a moment neither of them spoke; it was as if some silent message was spoken between them. Then the music ended and her father was speaking loudly over a microphone. Drew turned to listen to what he was saying and the spell was broken.

'Good evening, ladies and gentlemen.' Her father beamed at the crowd gathered around. 'I'm glad you've all been able to attend this special occasion. As I'm sure you are all aware, we are here to celebrate the new ownership of Hunter Fashions, and without further ado I'd like to introduce you to the new man in control—Mr Drew Sheldon.'

A spotlight swung to flood over Amanda and Drew. Drew smiled regretfully at her. 'I won't be long, Amanda.' His arm left her waist and he made his way through the crowds to the top of the room. Amanda felt strangely alone as she watched him go.

Drew took the microphone from her father and smiled. 'I want to thank you all for coming this evening, and Donald for throwing such a lovely party. There's another reason for celebration tonight—I have a surprise announcement to make.' He paused and his eyes searched the crowd as if he was looking for someone.

Out of the corner of her eye, Amanda saw Jordan making her way towards the front of the crowd and suddenly her blood ran cold. Was Drew going to announce their engagement? Had he changed his mind about keeping it a secret? Abruptly Amanda turned and jostled her way through the crowd; she had to get out of here. She couldn't bear to hear Drew telling everyone how much he loved Jordan, she couldn't clap or cheer or pretend she was pleased for them.

She noticed that the french doors at the end of the room were slightly open to let some fresh air into the crowded room, and on impulse she made towards them.

The night air was cool and refreshing against her fevered skin as she stepped outside. The garden was tranquil and beautiful, fairy-lights twinkling and reflecting in the large lily pond with its gushing fountain. She stood on the edge of the patio, savouring the solitude. Why did Drew take such pleasure in hurting her? It seemed almost cruel that he should want to tell everyone of his love for Jordan—here of all places, where they had danced and toasted their engagement with much the same crowd that were here tonight.

'You know, you should put something warmer on if you want to stand out here.' Drew's voice made her jump nervously. She didn't turn around, but continued to stare out into the darkness as if it held the answer to her worries.

'Leave me alone, Drew, go back inside and drink your champagne,' she said flatly.

'It's a little overcrowded for me in there.' She could hear his footsteps crossing the patio towards her. 'So I brought the champagne outside.' He was standing directly behind her now and he put one arm around her shoulders, handing her a crystal glass filled with the golden liquid. She stared at it for a moment and swallowed hard on a lump in her throat. 'Is this for me to toast your—your little announcement?' she asked in a dry voice. Somehow she just couldn't bring herself to even say the word 'engagement'.

'If you like.' She could hear the casual indifference in his voice, and anger and hurt jostled for position inside her. He really was a cold-hearted swine! She wanted to take the elegant glass and smash it on the cold concrete, screaming that no, she didn't like. But that was probably what he wanted her to do: it would feed his male ego to know that he had upset her so much. Presumably that was why he had followed her like this—to calculate her reaction and to gloat.

She took the glass from him with a hand that trembled slightly, although she fought hard to keep it steady. What

should she say? I hope you and Jordan will be very
happy? She dismissed that immediately; she would never
be able to say that with any semblance of unconcerned
aloofness.

'Here's to the future,' Drew murmured in her ear
before she could form any words.

'Yes—the future,' said Amanda numbly, and took a
sip of the sparkling liquid; it seemed to lodge awkwardly
in her throat, refusing to go down so that she felt she
was going to choke.

'I know we've had our differences in the past,
Amanda, but I hope we can forget them and work
together for the good of the company,' he said smoothly.

She swallowed convulsively. Did he imagine that she
was going to fly into a jealous rage and refuse to have
anything more to do with him because he was marrying
someone else? She would have to make it very clear that
she didn't give a damn. 'I've got more important things
to think about than the past,' she said calmly. 'As far
as I'm concerned, that was all over and done with long
ago.'

'I see.' There was a heavy silence for a moment. 'So
we can start afresh on good terms, then?'

'Of course,' she said lightly. 'After all, it is to my advantage to work well with you. It's not every day that
a designer gets the chance to launch her collection in
Paris.'

'And it's something you have always wanted,' he said
softly.

Amanda closed her eyes for a moment. So he did remember her telling him that. 'Yes.' Her voice was a mere
whisper in the stillness of the night.

'Now that I've appointed a manager for Hunter's, he'll
be able to take care of things this end. So you and I can
fly to Paris early next week.'

She stiffened; there was no way she wanted to go to
Paris with Drew! Her nerves jangled alarmingly at the

very thought. 'I don't think so, Drew—I've got such a lot to do here.'

'Nothing that can't be done from over there,' he dismissed abruptly. 'You're the only one who knows exactly what has to be done for the show.'

And what did Jordan think about his disappearing to Paris with another woman? she wondered suddenly. She remembered how she had felt when it had been her, and shivered violently.

'You're cold,' Drew murmured. She felt his hand cover her bare shoulder with a featherlight caress which sent her blood racing through her veins as if it were on fire. She wanted to pull sharply away from him, but she didn't dare move. 'That dress is very lovely, but it's not meant for standing outdoors in early spring.' He brought her back close against him so that she could feel the smooth material of his suit against her bare skin. The feeling was electric, and she flinched away from him, her body tensing with shock.

'Stop it, Drew.' Her voice rose unsteadily. 'All this phoney concern is making me feel sick. You and I both know that if I dropped down dead at your feet, your only concern would be that I hadn't finished working on the collection.'

'Oh, I don't know about that.' Drew traced a gentle finger down the satin-smooth skin of her back. 'There might be a few regrets for what might have been.'

'Don't you dare touch me!' She turned fiercely to look at him. 'And there was never any chance of anything between us except regrets.' She held back the tears with difficulty. Her eyes were large and glimmering like deep emeralds. She couldn't see the expression on his face, it was in darkness, his back against the light. No doubt he probably found her very amusing. He was probably smiling that taunting smile of his. That he should make fun of her like this really hurt. She ran a trembling hand through her hair and moved to go past him, back into the safety of the house.

He caught her arm in a vicelike grip. 'Not quite so fast; you and I haven't finished our little talk.'

'Oh, but we have.' She struggled to move away. 'There's nothing more I want to say to you—you're starting to bore me now.'

'Oh, am I, indeed?' He sounded furious now—that remark must have flayed at his male pride. 'Well, let's see if I can liven things up for you.' He pulled her roughly against him and lowered his head.

He's going to kiss me! she thought wildly, and her nerves screamed out against it. How dared he—how dared he treat her like this? First he publicly tried to humiliate her and hurt her, now he was going to kiss her without one ounce of feeling, just to make sure his lesson had struck home. She felt his breath warm against her lips and her champagne-glass slipped from helpless fingers down on to the concrete, smashing into a thousand splintered pieces beside them.

The noise brought Drew's head up sharply. 'Are you all right? You haven't hurt yourself?'

She felt like laughing hysterically. Of course she was hurt—but the crazy thing was she had no right to be: she had no claim to Drew, no reason to be jealous about Jordan. But she was incredibly jealous, very hurt. She shook her head. 'No.'

Without releasing her, his fingers touched her throat, resting gently on the hurried pulse that beat beneath the pale skin. Amanda stood very still. She knew the racing beat was giving her tumultuous emotions away to him and she needed to defend herself. 'That—that glass is very like our fragile working relationship: one false move and—smash, it's finished.'

'Is that some sort of threat?' His voice hardened.

'Call it what you like,' she shrugged. 'You may have blackmailed me into staying on at Hunter's, but you need me to launch the new boutique in Paris. Blackmail can work both ways, Drew.' Her voice sounded far more confident than she felt. 'So just keep your distance.'

The doors opened behind them and James called her name. Drew made no move to free her; instead he pulled her closer with almost punishing savagery. 'Get rid of him,' he growled angrily. 'Do it now.'

Her eyes widened at the imperious command. 'I'll do no such thing! You lost your right to tell me what to do the day I gave you my engagement ring back. Now I do exactly as I please.'

He shook his head. 'No, you do exactly as *I* please,' he corrected her. 'I'm going to have control over what you do and where you go from now on.' Abruptly he turned and left her, passing James silently.

Amanda was trembling with reaction. He had sounded so angry and bitter. In that instant she had seen past the smooth veneer to the man underneath. Drew was revelling in his power over her. His reasons for buying Hunter's were most probably business. Drew was first and foremost a businessman, but if he could hurt her a little along the way he would. He was not a man who would leave old scores unsettled.

'What the hell are you doing out here with him?' James moved over towards her a little unsteadily.

'Nothing. James, would you mind very much if we went home now?' She turned to look at him and came back to earth with a jolt. 'You're drunk!' Her voice was filled with dismay.

'Well, aren't you the observant one?' he drawled, his eyes narrowed into blue slits as he tried to focus on her. 'What's the matter, honey? I thought you were having a good time.'

'Not particularly.' She ran a shaky hand through her auburn hair and wondered what she was going to do with him. He was far too drunk to drive her home. 'I really would like to leave, but I think I'd better ring a taxi for us.'

'No way—I brought you and I'm taking you home.' He moved nearer and slipped as his foot made contact with the broken glass on the patio. Amanda caught hold of his arm to steady him.

'Are you all right?'

He shrugged her away. 'Perfectly,' he snapped angrily. 'Let's get out of here.' He moved towards the doors and she had no option but to follow him. She couldn't allow him to drive his car; he would kill himself or someone else.

She didn't know how James managed to get himself through the crowds inside. He was very unsteady on his feet. He must have drunk a lot once he had left her with Drew, although, now that she thought about it, he had been drinking constantly since the beginning of the evening.

Her heart sank as she went into the hall and saw Drew and Jordan talking with her father. Drew looked directly at her, cool and aloof. Her eyes dropped nervously away to rest for a moment on his beautiful fiancée. Her red dress was shimmering under the lights of the chandeliers, it moulded perfectly to her every curve. Amanda's expert eye for fashion placed it as a Dior. It was probably one of the little numbers that Drew had bought for her.

What kind of an engagement ring had he placed on her finger tonight? she wondered. A coldness surrounded her heart and she looked hurriedly away; she didn't want to see it.

Her father came over towards her, but the couple remained where they were, Drew leaning indolently against the curve of the mahogany staircase. A man went over towards them and she could hear him congratulating Drew in a loud, enthusiastic voice.

'You're not leaving so early, are you, darling?' her father asked. 'The party has only just got going.'

'I'm sorry, Dad, but I'm feeling very tired,' she said, and it wasn't just an excuse, she did feel drained all of a sudden.

'Well, I suppose you will need a couple of early nights before you jet off to Paris,' Donald smiled. 'This fashion show is a wonderful opportunity for you, Amanda.'

'Yes.' Her voice was noticeably lacking in enthusiasm.

'There's nothing wrong, is there?' her father frowned.

'No, of course not.' Amanda darted a glance towards James, who was struggling to open the front door. 'Look, I'll have to go, Dad. James has had rather a lot to drink, and I don't want him getting behind the wheel of his car.'

Donald Hunter shot a concerned glance towards the door. 'If you hang on for a while, I'll get my chauffeur to take you both home.'

Amanda shook her head firmly; she didn't want to hang around here any longer. Her father would probably expect her to stand making small talk with Drew. 'No, don't worry. I'll drive us home in James's car.'

'Will you be able to manage that powerful car in these twisty country lanes?' her father asked anxiously.

'No problem.' She reached to kiss his cheek. 'I'll ring you tomorrow.'

Would she be able to manage that car? she wondered nervously once she was outside. It was a long time since she had driven, and then it had only been in a little Mini. It was a far cry from the gleaming monster that James was standing next to now.

A cold wind rustled the trees beside them and sent heavy clouds sailing across the moon so that it was suddenly very dark. She shivered and wrapped her gossamer silk stole around her bare shoulders.

'James, please don't even attempt to drive that car,' she implored.

'I suppose you're creating all this fuss because you want to go home with Sheldon,' he jeered, rooting in his pockets for his key. 'Haven't you got any pride? Can't you realise even now that he doesn't give a damn about you?'

Amanda swallowed on a lump in her throat. 'This has nothing to do with Drew. Please, James, don't drive that car.'

'If you want to go home with Sheldon, then go,' he said persistently.

'Don't be childish.' She held out her hand as he found his key. 'If you insist on taking the car, then let me drive.'

'Childish?' He staggered back slightly. 'That's rich, coming from you! You could take the world trophy in naïveté. You haven't realised even now what a two-timing son of a——'

'James, that's enough,' she cut in sharply, anguish filling her voice.

Powerful headlights flooded over them as a silver Rolls-Royce pulled around the side of the house. It stopped beside them and an electric window wound down smoothly. 'Having problems?' Drew asked with sardonic amusement.

'Nothing I can't handle,' she said briskly, turning her attention back to James, hoping Drew would just drive on. The door slamming behind her and the crunch of his shoes on the gravel told her differently.

'That's not the story I got from your father,' he told her grimly as he walked towards James with a lithe, determined walk.

Amanda bit her lip. So her father had sent him after her. For some reason, having that bluntly pointed out to her made her furiously angry. 'Well, this is none of my father's or your damn business. So just go away.'

'That's right, Sheldon, go away,' James echoed her and sounded delighted. 'Before I knock your block off.'

Drew looked very amused at that. 'Well, I guess you owe me one.' He stood in front of James, towering over him. 'Go ahead.'

For a moment James looked completely nonplussed. 'Well, you asked for it.' He staggered back and took a wild swing which Drew had no trouble in sidestepping, allowing James to go sprawling on the grass.

'James!' Horrified, Amanda rushed over to him. 'Are you all right?' There was no answer and she shook his inert body. 'I think you've really hurt him!' She glared up at Drew accusingly.

'I didn't touch him, and he deserves anything he gets,' he grated harshly. 'If there's one thing I can't stand it's a fool who thinks he can drink and drive.' He looked down at him with unconcerned eyes. 'Open the back door of the Rolls, Amanda. I suppose we'll have to get him home.'

Amanda hesitated, about to argue. Then she changed her mind. If she said anything he would probably leave James to spend the night outdoors. She retrieved the bunch of keys James had dropped on the ground, then watched as Drew lifted James easily over one shoulder and deposited him on the back seat of the Rolls as if he were a sack of potatoes.

'He's going to have one hell of a hangover tomorrow,' he observed wryly as James slumped down without stirring.

'He will be all right, won't he?' Amanda shivered as the wind ruffled her red-gold hair.

'Yes, I regret to say.' Drew opened the front passenger door for her. 'He doesn't deserve your concern, he could have killed you tonight.' His dark features looked grim and angry in the moonlight. Amanda got into the car without answering him.

They drove back to the city in silence, Drew's hands manipulating the wheel and the gear-changes with skilful ease. She watched his powerful hands and remembered, without wanting to, how wonderful they had once felt against the softness of her skin, how he had caressed her to heights of almost unbearable pleasure.

The city towered up out of the darkness and they were in among the lights and traffic and crowds of people.

'Where do you want me to drop him?' Drew bit out the question roughly as if to say he knew where he would *like* to drop him.

She gave him the address of his apartment calmly. She supposed she couldn't really blame him for being angry with her. He couldn't have wanted to leave his fiancée in the middle of their celebrations. Doubtless he wanted to get rid of them as fast as possible and get back to her.

'Is your passport in order?' Drew asked her suddenly.

'Yes, but...'

'No buts, Amanda, we leave for Paris first thing Monday morning,' he told her firmly. He slowed the car outside James's apartment. 'Stay here,' he ordered briskly, 'while I dispose of the body.'

Resenting the overbearing way he was ordering her around, Amanda got out of the car with him.

'I'll open the doors for you,' she told him as he shot her an angry frown.

'You surely don't want to spend the night with him in this condition! He won't be much use to you,' he said caustically.

Her cheeks flamed red at the suggestion in his words.

'You're blushing!' he observed with dry amusement as he bent to lift James up.

'Well, that remark was crude and insulting,' she said sharply.

James seemed to be coming round, and somehow he managed to stagger upstairs, heavily supported by Drew.

'Shall I make him some black coffee?' she asked as they put him down on his large double bed.

'I think we've done enough for him.' Drew walked over to look more closely at some pictures on the wall. They were the ones James had taken of her in the Lake District. Beautiful, dreamy photographs that looked very romantic.

'He's captured you perfectly,' Drew murmured as he studied the one of her in the white summer ballgown, the sun catching her hair so that it gleamed a deep, fiery gold.

IT'S FUN! IT'S FREE!
AND YOU COULD BE A
MILLIONAIRE!

Your unique Sweepstakes Entry Number appears on the Sweepstakes Entry Form. When you affix your Sweepstakes Entry Sticker to your Form, you're in the running, and you could be the $1,000,000.00 annuity Grand Prize Winner! That's $33,333.33 every year for up to 30 years!

AFFIX BONUS PRIZE STICKER

to your Sweepstakes Entry Form. If you have a winning number, you could collect any of 8,617 prizes. And we'll also enter you in a special bonus prize drawing for a new Ford Mustang and the "Aloha Hawaii Vacation."

AFFIX FREE BOOKS AND GIFTS STICKER

to take advantage of our Free Books/Free Gifts introduction to the Harlequin Reader Service®. You'll get four brand new Harlequin Presents® novels, plus a 20kt gold electroplated necklace and a mystery gift, absolutely free!

NO PURCHASE NECESSARY!

Accepting free books and gifts places you under no obligation to buy a thing! After receiving your free books, if you don't wish to receive any further volumes, write "cancel" on the shipping document and return it to us. But if you choose to remain a member of the Harlequin Reader Service, you'll receive six more Harlequin Presents novels every month for just $2.24* each—26 cents below the cover price, with no additional charge for delivery! You can cancel at any time by dropping us a line, or by returning a shipment to us at our cost. Even if you cancel, your first four books, your 20kt gold electroplated chain and your mystery gift are absolutely free—our way of thanking you for giving the Reader Service a try!

* Terms and prices subject to change without notice.
  Sales tax applicable in N.Y. and Iowa   ©1990 HARLEQUIN ENTERPRISES LTD.

You'll love your elegant 20kt gold electro-plated chain! The necklace is finely crafted with 160 double-soldered links and is electro-plate finished in genuine 20kt gold. And it's free as added thanks for giving our Reader Service a try!

Harlequin Reader Service® Sweepstakes Entry Form

This is your **unique** Sweepstakes Entry Number: 3K 499205

> This could be your lucky day! If you have the winning number, you could be the Grand Prize Winner. To be eligible, *affix Sweepstakes Entry Sticker here!*

> If you would like a chance to win the $25,000.00 prize, the $10,000.00 prize, or one of the many $5,000.00, $1,000.00, $250.00 or $10.00 prizes…plus the Mustang and the Hawaiian Vacation, *affix Bonus Prize Sticker here!*

> To receive free books and gifts with no obligation to buy, as explained on the opposite page, *affix the Free Books and Gifts Sticker here!*

Please enter me in the sweepstakes and, when the winner is drawn, tell me if I've won the $1,000,000.00 Grand Prize! Also tell me if I've won any other prize, including the car and the vacation prize. Please ship me the free books and gifts I've requested with sticker above. Entering the Sweepstakes costs me nothing and places me under no obligation to buy! (If you do not wish to receive free books and gifts, do not affix the FREE BOOKS and GIFTS sticker.)

106 CIH BA6F
(U-H-P-08/90)

YOUR NAME   PLEASE PRINT

ADDRESS   APT#

CITY   STATE   ZIP

Offer limited to one per household and not valid for current Harlequin Presents subscribers.

Printed in U.S.A.   © 1990 Harlequin Enterprises Ltd

DETACH AND MAIL TODAY

Harlequin's "No Risk" Guarantee

- You're not required to buy a single book — ever!
- As a subscriber, you must be completely satisfied or you may cancel at any time by marking "cancel" on your statement or returning a shipment of books at our cost.
- The free books and gifts you receive are yours to keep.

**If card is missing, write to: Harlequin Reader Service,
P.O. Box 1867, Buffalo, NY 14269-1867**

Printed in U.S.A.

DETACH AND MAIL TODAY

POSTAGE WILL BE PAID BY ADDRESSEE

BUSINESS REPLY MAIL
FIRST CLASS MAIL   PERMIT NO. 717   BUFFALO, NY

HARLEQUIN READER SERVICE
PO BOX 1867
BUFFALO NY 14240-9952

NO POSTAGE
NECESSARY
IF MAILED
IN THE
UNITED STATES

'He's a good photographer,' said Amanda without glancing at them. 'That's why you offered him the job in Bermuda, isn't it?'

'Partly.' He turned towards her. 'I suppose you've seen these before?' His eyes seemed to burn straight through her.

'Of course.' It was only after she had answered him that she realised what he was driving at. He was really asking if she had been in his bedroom before!

There was an electric silence and Amanda glared at him. She was damned if she was going to tell him that she had never set foot inside James's apartment before. It was none of his business.

'What do you mean, partly?' Her eyes narrowed suspiciously. 'You either offered it to him because you thought he'd do a good job, or you didn't.'

'Oh, he'd do a good job all right.' Drew's eyes never left her face. 'But the main reason I offered it to him was to get him out of your hair.'

'What?' All the colour drained from Amanda's face. So James had been partly right, after all.

'You heard.' Drew's voice was stony cold. 'You can't concentrate properly on your work while that idiot's around, sending you flowers, phoning you at the office, waltzing into your house where designs are lying around.'

'How dare you?' Amanda blazed. 'You have no right to interfere in my private life. Who the hell do you think you are?'

'Your boss,' he said flatly. 'The man who's pouring a million pounds into your career. I don't want everything ruined with one careless slip of the tongue. This collection is top secret and top priority. It should be the most important thing in your life right now.'

'Not everyone can cast their feelings aside for their work,' she flung at him bitterly. 'Not everyone can be as cold-blooded and ruthless as you.'

His eyes narrowed on her. 'You haven't begun to find out just how ruthless I can be.'

She shivered at the hard, steely tone and stared at him in disbelief.

'Now, let's get out of here.' Drew held open the door, and with one quick glance to make sure James was sleeping peacefully she complied. That tone wasn't one she wanted to argue with.

Drew didn't speak again until he reached her house. 'I'll pick you up seven o'clock sharp Monday morning. Be ready.'

She turned away from him and opened the door.

'I'm warning you, Amanda. You've broken one agreement with me. Break another at your peril.'

The words made her shiver as she stood in the darkness of the night and watched the powerful car accelerate away from her.

CHAPTER SEVEN

AMANDA was ready early in the morning. She had her cases packed and waiting at six-thirty.

She was wearing a stylish cream wool suit teamed with a silk blouse in the most delicate tone of peach. Her hair shone like gold as the early-morning sun slanted over her. She had just finished plaiting it in a long, thick braid down her back, and now she sat down to sip her black coffee and prepare herself mentally for the day ahead.

She'd had a lot of time over the weekend to think about things—especially Drew's engagement. Strange how that one thought had clouded her mind completely over the last few days, overriding every other emotion. She had spoken to her father on the phone for a brief time and he had talked endlessly about how wonderful Drew was and what a fantastic career opportunity he was giving her. Her father was a little like Drew in some ways: work always got top priority, there wasn't a lot of room for sentiment. At least he had been tactful enough not to mention Drew's engagement, or maybe he hadn't even given it a thought. Whatever the reason, Amanda had been grateful, she couldn't bear to talk about it. She could hardly endure thinking about it.

It wasn't that she was jealous, she thought sharply. It was just the hurtful way Drew had done everything. She didn't care who he married; in fact, she felt sorry for Jordan. Drew would never be the faithful type; he held a dangerous attraction for women and he knew it. Jordan would probably have to put up with one casual affair after another.

The doorbell rang and her cup rattled precariously against the saucer as she put it down on the table. She was trembling, suddenly afraid of seeing him, of trying to talk to him in a casual, indifferent way. How on earth was she going to be able to work for a man who could wreak such havoc inside her?

She took a deep breath before opening the door. 'Hello, Drew.' She couldn't bring herself to look at him, but moved to pick up her jacket from the chair.

'Are you ready?' He sounded surprised and she turned to glance at him, immediately regretting the impulse as her eyes locked on his powerfully handsome physique.

He was wearing a dark grey suit which was tailored perfectly over his broad-shouldered frame. His shirt was white and crisp against his tanned skin

'I—I think so,' she murmured. Inside, her nerves twisted into tight knots. She didn't want to go away with him, her every instinct was telling her that being in close contact with him was going to have disastrous consequences.

'Got your passport?' he asked, coming to pick up her bags.

She nodded and stepped nervously out of his way.

'Good, that's all that matters. We can buy anything else you need.' His eyes flicked over her appraisingly for a moment before he bent and picked up her cases. 'Right, let's go, then,' he said in a crisp tone.

Amanda had never felt more nervous as she sat next to him in the back of his long, sleek limousine. The argument they'd had on Friday evening seemed to be hanging in the air between them, making the silence crackle with electricity. She wished she could break the unbearable tension, but what could she say? Did you and Jordan have a good weekend? No—better to keep away from anything personal. She should talk about business; after all, this was a business trip.

'Have you seen anything of James this weekend?' asked Drew suddenly.

She frowned. 'Why? Is it not allowed?' Immediately she regretted the sharp retort. Things would never be businesslike between them if she continued to snipe at him like this. 'He phoned Saturday morning, he wasn't feeling very well,' she told him hastily. In actual fact, James had been feeling very sorry for himself.

'Did he tell you he's accepted my offer of work in Bermuda?' Drew slanted her a deeply probing look.

'Yes, he told me.' Amanda turned her head and looked out at the grey London streets. 'I hope you're going to treat him fairly.'

'I treat all my staff fairly,' Drew growled.

'Except those who have displeased you in some way in the past,' she said quietly.

'For God's sake, Amanda, I'm taking you to Paris to arrange a fashion show, not to the guillotine!' There was a note of exasperation in his voice now.

'I'm very grateful for this marvellous opportunity,' she said in a dutiful voice.

'I don't want your gratitude,' he bit out sharply. 'Only your co-operation.'

She nodded. 'Well, maybe if we can both put aside the fact that we despise each other, there might be some chance for that.'

'Maybe,' he agreed softly.

The limousine pulled up smoothly outside the airport entrance and the chauffeur came around to open the door for them. Drew climbed out and reached down to hand her out while the chauffeur went to deal with the luggage.

Amanda found Drew's hand on her arm unsettling, and made to pull away from him. Only she lost her balance, and Drew's arms went automatically around her to steady her. 'I—I'm sorry.' She gasped a little at the pressure of his body so close to hers and looked upwards to the strong features of his face, feeling a little dazed.

It was then that the flash of a camera lit the grey morning, catching them unawares. Drew swore slightly under his breath as a group of reporters jostled and pushed around them, bombarding them with questions. Some about Drew's takeover of Hunter Fashions, some insultingly personal about his past relationship with Amanda. She flinched uncomfortably and turned her head away from the prying eyes of the newsmen. It was obvious that the story of Drew's engagement hadn't broken yet, because there was no reference to it. When it did they would really have a field day, she thought miserably.

Drew put an arm around her and drew her close against his side protectively, answering their questions with the casual ease of a man accustomed to dealing with the press. At the same time he guided her skilfully through them.

When asked directly if they were having an affair, Drew smiled in a relaxed manner. 'Amanda and I are partners in business only.' He half turned to face them as they reached the door through to the first-class departure lounge. 'However, as you can see, negotiations are under way to rectify that.' As they all smiled and took note of his comments, Drew quickly slipped them through the doors and away from the reporters.

Amanda turned to face him immediately, her face flushed a bright, angry red. 'How dare you? How dare you insinuate that we are—are——' She floundered to a halt, too angry to think straight.

His lips curved in wry amusement. 'My dear Amanda, there's nothing for you to get so steamed up about. You've got to learn early on how to use the Press, because they sure as hell use you.'

She was staring at him, bemused. 'But it will be all over London tomorrow that we're having an affair! What will everyone think after—after the way you behaved on Friday night?'

He smiled slightly. 'I thought I behaved like a perfect gentleman on Friday night. I don't think I gave anyone any reason to complain.' He caught hold of her arm as she looked set to explode. 'Don't look so serious. There's nothing like a little scandal to get wonderful free publicity for the fashion house. It's when people stop talking that you've got to worry.'

She glared at him fiercely. 'I don't care about you using the Press, but I do object when you start using me in your sordid little schemes!'

'If it's James you're worrying about—don't.' Drew started to move across the room, bringing her with him. 'I'm sure he'll read between the lines and see it as a publicity stunt.'

As Jordan would, presumed Amanda angrily. 'Did you arrange for them to be here?' she asked, suddenly suspicious.

'No, somebody from our promotions company probably tipped them off. We need as much publicity as we can get. Stop fretting, Amanda, they'll print a completely different story next week in all probability.'

Well, of course they would, Amanda thought angrily. Next week they would probably know that he was going to marry Jordan.

Once they had settled themselves in the comfortable executive-class seats of the plane, Drew opened his briefcase and proceeded to work. Amanda glanced idly through a fashion magazine, her eyes often straying to his intent profile. He was so self-possessed, so sure of himself. When Drew made up his mind that he wanted something, he always got it. Her lips curved in a half-smile. The odds against her sitting on this plane with him would have been a thousand to one last week, yet here she was. He had an aura of power and grim determination that made saying no to him almost impossible. She had noticed that strength in him from the moment she had first set eyes on him; it was dangerous, exciting, sensual. All the things that made a woman's heartbeat quicken and ache with longing. Jordan would probably miss him terribly while he was away. Or maybe she would be far too busy arranging things for the wedding. Would she fly over to Paris to choose her wedding dress from the collection? It would be ironic if she chose the very dress Amanda had designed for her own wedding!

She turned her head towards Drew, and suddenly her eyes were wide and filled with anguish.

'Drew, I've suddenly remembered that I've included a dress in the collection that shouldn't be there,' she told him breathlessly.

He looked up from his papers. 'Oh?' His eyes raked over her face. 'Which dress?'

'One of the last designs among the ones I gave you at the office.' Her hands twisted in distress; she had to have that dress back, she couldn't leave it. It was crazy, but the thought of Jordan wearing that dress for Drew made her feel positively nauseous with jealousy.

His eyes narrowed, his face suddenly became grim. 'Why do you want it?'

She hesitated and then decided to tell the truth; after all, he needn't know she had designed it for their wedding. 'It's mine—I designed it for myself.'

'I see.' He looked back down at his papers and for a moment she didn't think he was going to say any more on the subject.

'So you will give it back to me?' she went on.

He looked at her then, his eyes hard. 'You don't love him, so why are you going to marry him?' he asked harshly.

She stared at him, bewildered for a moment until suddenly it became clear: he thought the dress was for her marriage to James! 'I had no idea you were such an expert on other people's affairs,' she managed to say coolly. 'Will you give me the dress back?'

'I'll see.' He flicked back over his work impatiently and she didn't dare say any more, he sounded so remote and unapproachable. Maybe it was a good thing to let him believe she was serious about James. It would give her something to hide behind, and she had a feeling she was going to need very strong barriers to be able to survive life working for him.

The hotel's chauffeured Mercedes Benz met them outside Charles de Gaulle airport and swept them away through the bustling, impatient traffic of Paris.

Although she tried hard to remain detached and cool about everything, it was hard not to show her excitement as she looked out at the boulevards and the beauty of the old buildings with their shutters wide open to the golden sunshine. She pushed the button to wind down the electric windows, breathing in the soft spring air with enjoyment. The sharp breeze ruffled her hair, allowing a few stray tendrils of her hair to curl around her face.

'Sorry, am I distracting you?' She turned wide green eyes on Drew, who was still studying documents. He had hardly said two words to her since their brief conversation in the plane. He had been immersed in his work, his face dark and grim as he sorted through something that was obviously making his temper fray at the edges.

'You always distract me,' he said with a wry curve of his lips as his gaze travelled over her auburn hair to her long legs.

'I'm sorry.' A bright flush lit her face as she hastily wound the window back up again.

Drew put his papers back inside his briefcase and resolutely snapped it shut. 'It doesn't matter, I've nearly finished anyway.' He turned a little in his seat to give her his full attention. 'We've got a lot of work to get through in the next few weeks.'

'Have you set a date yet for the show?' she asked with interest.

'Yes,' he smiled. 'April the twenty-second.'

Her eyes widened in horror. 'We'll never be ready in time! It'll be impossible to arrange a complete show in that time, plus the fact that the last few designs only left the drawing-board last week.'

'There's no such word as impossible in my vocabulary,' he told her easily. 'But we're going to have to pull together. What I'm saying, Amanda, is that we

should forget our differences and pour all that energy
into the collection. We used to get on so well together,
so there's no reason why we can't again if we both give
it our best try.' He gave a lopsided grin that made her
heart flutter madly. 'What do you say—shall we call a
truce?'

She nodded and found herself smiling back at him.
He could be so charming when he wanted to be, and
that smile of his was so endearing. When he looked at
her like that it was hard to think straight, never mind
argue. 'Yes, truce,' she said softly.

The car pulled up outside the imposing entrance to
the Sheldon Hotel and they stepped out into the bright
sunlight. A porter came down the steps and took their
cases from the driver while they went into the quiet and
luxurious foyer. They crossed the thick red carpets
towards the reception desk, where a young French girl
smiled respectfully at Drew as he spoke to her in perfect
French.

There was soon a flurry of excitement around the desk
as various staff realised that the boss had arrived and
strove to accommodate him with super-efficiency.

Amanda let her gaze wander around the sumptuous
interior of the Sheldon. It was an enormous hotel, an
impressive mixture of period opulence and modern
luxury, for although it had been extensively modernised
it still retained its calm, dignified character. A majestic
white marble staircase swept upwards, leading her eye
to the 1930s stained-glass windows which still filtered
the Parisian sunlight through giant sunflowers and roses.
Chandeliers caught the colourful light and shimmered
like a million diamonds suspended on golden skeins.

Amanda turned her attention as the manager of the
hotel appeared and Drew spoke to him in rapid French.
The manager was a lot older than Drew, but it was obvious by the Frenchman's attitude of genuine atten-
tiveness when Drew spoke that he respected his boss very
much.

She allowed her glance to linger on Drew's arresting profile, the high cheekbones and determinedly rugged jawline. His firm mouth was curved in a sudden smile. What was it about him that stirred her so deeply? She loved the sound of his voice speaking French; the rich, deep intonations set her blood on fire. She hadn't realised that he could speak the language so fluently, but then she didn't really know very much about him at all. Even though they had once been lovers, he had always kept a part of him locked away from her. She felt a deep shaft of pain hit her and wondered miserably why that should still hurt her.

Drew turned to introduce the Frenchman to her and she quickly pulled herself together. She might have made a peace pact with Drew, but she was going to have to be very careful not to be lulled into a false sense of security. She would have to keep her distance.

A little while later, when they stepped out of the private lift into the most sumptuous lounge Amanda had ever set foot in, she realised that keeping her distance was going to be harder than she had anticipated.

'Is this your private apartment?' she asked him nervously.

'It is.' He put his briefcase down and crossed the room towards the long windows, which completely covered one wall. The blinds were drawn on them, throwing the room into shade.

'Where—where am I to sleep?' she asked, a little self-consciously.

'Don't worry, you'll have your own private room.' She could hear the smile in his voice and could feel the beginnings of anger inside her. She wanted to make some sarcastic reply, but she bit her lip and turned to look more closely at the room instead. If she said anything now their truce would have lasted all of one hour.

The lounge was exquisitely furnished. An opulent white carpet and white walls made a dramatic background for the black circular settee and chairs and the

bold, contemporary paintings. A log fire burnt brightly
in a black marble fireplace, throwing flickering shadows
until Drew pulled the blinds back and sunlight flooded
over everything.

Amanda gasped at the view outside. Now that the
blinds were back she could see they had covered sliding
glass doors, not windows, and they led out on to a spectacular rooftop garden with a view out over the skyline
of Paris. The garden was like a private country retreat
in the midst of the city. The grass was smooth and perfectly manicured, and in the centre a large swimming
pool shimmered dazzlingly in the golden light of the sun.

Drew smiled at her. 'It's a lovely view of Paris, isn't
it?' He pulled the doors open. 'Come and have a look.'
He waited for her to move past and then joined her
outside. She walked towards the very edge of the roof
and leaned her elbows on the concrete parapet.

The roof had a commanding view out over Paris, and
it was breathtaking. She could see the Champs-Elysées,
and, just visible, the Arc de Triomphe, which even from
the distance looked majestic, elevated slightly over the
traffic which looked like little toys going up towards it.

She stood silently drinking in everything, trying to
store everything in her memory. She was so enthralled
that she didn't notice Drew watching her with almost
the same intensity. The sunlight was catching the deep
golden texture of her hair; it was a striking foil against
her creamy skin and wide, bewitching green eyes.

'I could stand here all day; it's unbelievably beautiful.'
She turned those eyes towards him now, smiling in
excitement.

'So could I,' he agreed lazily. 'Tell me, Amanda, have
you visited Paris before?'

She nodded. 'Yes, once. But it was a flying visit and
I didn't get to see much of the sights. It was when I was
studying design at art college. We came to see a collection by Guy Laroche. It was a spectacular show, but
I was disappointed not to have seen more of Paris.'

'Maybe we should make some time to show you a few of the sights,' Drew murmured lazily.

About to jump enthusiastically at the chance, Amanda suddenly changed her mind. She was here to work, not go on pleasure trips with Drew; getting friendly with him could be very risky indeed. 'I think we should concentrate on work, don't you?' she said lightly.

Drew's mouth pulled into a straight line, but he shrugged casually. 'Yes, you're probably right.' He glanced at his gold wristwatch. 'Talking of work, I'd better go down to the offices and see what's been going on in my absence.'

'Shall I come with you?' she asked, unsure of what he expected from her.

'No, you relax and get your bearings today. Have a lie-down for a couple of hours; I'm sure you could do with it after our early start this morning.' He started to move back inside.

What about you? she felt like asking. After all, he had started early this morning as well, and he had worked non-stop during the journey. If he was able to get straight into his work here, why shouldn't she? 'I'd really prefer to do something,' she said, following him.

He shot her a considering look. 'I'll send someone up to give you a guided tour of the hotel later on. But I really don't want you overdoing it on your first day.'

Without giving her a chance to argue he left quickly by the main door, leaving her standing in the middle of the lounge. For a moment she felt like going after him; that last remark had sounded dangerously like an order, and she wasn't going to take any more of those from him. Then she let out her breath in a sigh. What was the point? He probably wouldn't take any notice of her anyway. She might as well unpack her clothes and take a shower. She looked around the room and realised that Drew hadn't told her where her room was. There were several doors leading off the lounge, the main one to the lift and two on either side of the room. She walked across to one and opened it. It led to an elegant dining-room and, just beyond, an ultra-modern kitchen. She closed the door—obviously the bedrooms were situated at the far side of the apartment. Sure enough, the door at the other side led to a long corridor and she moved down it, gently pushing open the doors to find out which one she had been allocated.

She found Drew's first. For a moment she let her eyes linger curiously on the palatial splendour of his private domain. The décor was all done in varying shades of blue. Polished rosewood furniture sat on a rich royal blue carpet. The french doors, which gave a glimpse of the palm trees in the garden and the sparkling pool, were curtained in a pale blue brocade. Drew's luggage was sitting neatly at the end of the king-sized bed, where the blue watered silk covers were folded back invitingly. This was probably the room Jordan had shared with him during those so-called business trips last year. Amanda turned away, angry with herself for thinking about that.

Her bedroom was directly next door. It was huge and luxuriously furnished, all toned in delicate shell-pinks and smoky china-blue. Behind the large brass bed with its pink satin pillows shaped like sea-shells, the french doors opened out directly on to the pool area.

She moved to unpack her cases which had been placed at one side of the bed; however, someone had already done it for her. Her clothes were all hanging neatly in the white, louvred fitted wardrobes. Amanda's eye-brows lifted slightly; she was used to doing things like that for herself. With a little shrug she selected a mint-green dress to change into and then crossed towards the adjoining bathroom. This was almost as large as the bedroom, a myriad mirrors reflecting the large, circular bath shaped like a giant sea-shell with ornate golden trimmings. There was a selection of perfumed bath oils and foams sitting next to the taps. Suddenly she dismissed the idea of a brisk shower and ran the water into the bath. She chose a lightly fragrant Dior to make the water silky and, taking off her clothes, climbed in with a sigh. Drew was right, she thought as she leaned her head back, I do need to relax for a little while.

Amanda felt very refreshed as she dried her auburn hair later and brushed it so that it glowed vibrantly against the green of her dress. She had slept for a while after her bath and, even though she had only had a couple of hours, it had done her the world of good. She hadn't been sleeping very well over the last few nights and she hadn't realised just how tired she was.

A knock at the door distracted her thoughts and she left her room to see who it was. The hotel manager stood just outside the main door to the suite. He smiled politely at her. 'Monsieur Sheldon has asked me to look in on you,' he said in his perfect English. 'Would you like room service to send you up some food?'

Amanda shook her head and declined. She had wasted enough time, and she felt she should be doing something useful now. 'Perhaps you would be kind enough to show me down to the offices?' she asked instead.

He agreed immediately. 'Yes, but of course. Monsieur Sheldon did ask that I familiarise you with the layout of the hotel.'

Amanda smiled. 'Right, well, I'll just get my bag. I won't be a moment.'

The hotel manager seemed to enjoy showing her around; it was obvious that he took a great pride in the impressive hotel.

'The Sheldon has everything, it is the most sophisticated and elegant hotel in Paris,' he told her as they wandered around the third floor which was completely devoted to guest amenities. There was a large, attractive swimming pool flanked by a jacuzzi in a tropical setting of greenery and flowers. In addition there was a gym, a sauna and beauty salon, a library, and even a business centre which offered executive and secretarial services.

'There must be a tremendous amount of work in running a hotel of this size,' said Amanda as they got back into the lift to go down to the ground-floor offices.

'Yes, but it runs smoothly. Monsieur Sheldon manages to come and run an eye over everything quite regularly. His office is always open to any of his staff who want to talk with him.' He smiled at Amanda. 'He is a man of decided views and forceful opinions, but he treats his staff fairly. Despite the size of his empire, he takes a personal interest in everything.'

The lift doors opened and, as they stepped out, Amanda could hear the sound of builders at work. 'Ah, now I must show you the new fashion salon that we are building.' The little Frenchman's eyes gleamed with excitement as he led her down the wide corridor. 'You will be interested in this, no doubt, as it is to be the show place for your creations.'

As they rounded a corner Amanda had a clear view of the new salon. It was large—very large, and, even though it wasn't finished, already it was impressive.

'Drew certainly doesn't do anything by half measures,' she breathed as she stood in the open doorway. There was still a lot of work to be done; floorboards were up and in the depths below there was a mass of tangled wires and plumbing. Drew was having a very elaborate lighting system put in by the looks of it, with spectacular fountains and a black spiral staircase leading to an upper balcony.

As Amanda stood trying to take it all in, a few of the workers noticed her and abruptly heads turned and work ceased in appreciation of the alluring female with long legs and glorious flame-coloured hair. There was a chorus of wolf-whistles and remarks shouted in French, which, even though she couldn't understand them, managed to bring a flush of colour to her delicate features.

A door opened a little way down the corridor and suddenly everyone was deeply engrossed in their work again. Turning, Amanda understood the quick change in the men as she saw Drew standing in the doorway.

'I thought it must be you,' he said with a grin. 'You'd better come into the office, I'm having difficulty keeping those men working as it is, without you distracting them.'

Her heart beating wildly, Amanda turned to obey him, thanking the manager for his time as he also turned to leave.

Drew's eyes raked over her as she came towards him. 'One thing I'll say for those men,' he said in a low voice, 'they have taste when it comes to recognising beautiful women.'

Amanda looked at him, uncertain how she should take such a compliment. His face was expressionless; maybe he felt that their delicate new truce meant that he had to throw in a few token flattering remarks. He stepped back to allow her to precede him into the beautifully furnished and thickly carpeted room which looked more like a luxurious sitting-room than an office. Only the large desks with computers defined it as a work-place.

There were four other people in the room, and they all looked up as she entered.

'Claude, Françoise, Roger, and Marion, your creative assistant.'

Drew introduced them. Amanda smiled at each of them; they were all around her own age, both the men dressed in very smart designer suits. Marion also wore what looked like a man's suit, only at her neck a large red silk bow broke the severity of the outfit. The French girl's dark hair was cut in a gleaming bob, and it swung silkily as the girl started to talk to her in rapid, excited French.

Drew held up a hand to interrupt her. 'I think for Amanda's sake we should all speak English from now on, otherwise we're going to run into difficulties.'

The girl's scarlet lips curved in a rueful smile. 'I beg your pardon, *mademoiselle*. I was just saying how excited we all are to be working with you on your collection.'

'Thank you,' Amanda smiled. 'And please call me Amanda.'

'Pour Amanda a cup of coffee, will you, Marion?' Drew said, moving behind his desk again. 'Now, where were we?'

Over the next few hours talk centred completely on the fashion show. Ideas were discussed heatedly and Françoise took copious notes on the ones agreed.

'Lastly, I have a pile of letters here from various magazines and publications,' Claude told Drew, running an impatient hand through his dark hair. 'They all are asking for interviews with you and Amanda.'

'We don't really have time for that,' Drew said, frowning. 'Are they worth considering?'

'Quite a few.' Claude went on to list a few very high-ranking fashion publications.

Drew pursed his lips thoughtfully. 'All right, we'll give one,' he said decisively. 'Get in touch with *Jours de France*. Tell them we'll give them an exclusive some time.' He looked directly at Amanda. 'They shouldn't get too personal; they'll only ask about the collection. Probably want a picture of the two of us together, that sort of thing.'

She nodded, aware that he was thinking about how angry she had got over the incident at the airport. It gave her a warm glow inside to know he had been considering her when he had chosen that particular magazine.

'Have you eaten yet, Amanda?' Drew asked her suddenly.

She shook her head, wondering with a strange little lurch of her heart if he was going to suggest they have dinner together.

'Why don't you and Marion finish now and go and have dinner?' he suggested lightly.

'Good idea,' Marion agreed immediately.

As they left the offices, Amanda tried to tell herself that she wasn't disappointed, that she hadn't really wanted Drew's company. But somewhere deep down she knew that she was kidding herself.

CHAPTER EIGHT

DURING the next week there wasn't time to think too deeply about anything except work. Amanda started at eight-thirty in the morning, and Drew was always already in the office when she arrived.

'Dynamic' was the only word that could describe Drew. She had never met a man with such driving, forceful energy. They all worked long, hard hours, but Drew did twice as much and he never seemed to be tired. When everyone looked exhausted at the end of the day he told them they had done too much, yet when they left he was still sitting at his desk. Sometimes he didn't arrive back into the apartment until the early hours of the morning.

He was an amazing boss to work for; nothing perturbed him. He was always patient and cool, and even in the most stressful of situations he managed to sort things out and still retain his sense of humour while he was doing it. Everyone admired him, respected him, and Amanda was no exception. Only, with her, the feelings ran deeper. Sometimes she would look at him across the room and try to understand why she should feel that dizzy, light-headed feeling when he smiled at her. Or why her heart seemed to beat out of control if he casually placed a hand on her shoulder or stood too close.

On Friday morning, when he handed her a stack of portfolios to look through so that she could start deciding on the models they would use, his hand accidentally brushed hers and she jumped as if she had received an electric shock, dropping everything on to the floor.

'Gosh, I'm sorry!' Horrified, she bent quickly to start picking them up with fingers that trembled alarmingly.

'No harm done.' Drew dropped down quickly to help her. 'Are you all right?' he asked casually, but she knew his sharp eyes had taken in her flustered state.

'Just a little on edge about the interview this afternoon,' she said, thanking heaven that she had some excuse to hide behind. 'I haven't had time to give any thought to what I should wear or how I should do my hair,' she added for good measure. Now he probably thinks I'm a neurotic woman, she thought with irritation.

'You'll look good no matter what you wear,' Drew told her easily, and took the folders from her. 'Why don't you take the rest of the morning off and relax?'

'No, really, that isn't necessary,' she told him hastily. 'I'd rather be fully occupied and not have time to think about it.'

Drew wasn't about to take no for an answer. 'Go up to the beauty salon. They'll keep you occupied and you can relax at the same time.' He opened the door and pointed her firmly towards it.

Amanda did indeed feel wonderful after a morning being pampered in the hotel's beauty salon. She was encased in hot wax to make her skin even softer, then massaged from head to toe. Then, as the stylist was attending to her hair, her nails were manicured, and a make-up artist cleverly enhanced her features with a minimum amount of effort. All that remained for her to do was to step into her clothes and she was ready to face a barrage of interviewers and photographers.

She chose one of her own designs, a black and white ensemble. The satin blouse had fine black stripes and crossed over in a plunging V neckline. It tied around the waist in a thick cummerbund with the stripes going in opposite directions, emphasising her narrow waist. The skirt was straight and plain black, cleverly cut to softly mould to her curves and flare out just below the knee. She wore no jewellery; the whole look was understated and very elegant.

'They're on their way up,' Drew informed her as she stepped out of her bedroom. His eyes lingered on her approvingly for a moment, before he went on in a businesslike tone, 'I thought it better if they interviewed us in the apartment, then we can have complete privacy.'

Amanda nodded, noticing that he had made a quick change into a midnight-blue suit which emphasised his dark good looks.

There was a knock on the door and Drew smiled at her. 'Before I let them in, have I told you how terrific you look?'

She grinned. 'Thank you. You don't look bad, either.'

There was another impatient knock on the door, and Drew's eyebrows rose. 'Well, I suppose I'd better let the rabble in, before they break the door down,' he said, moving to answer it. 'Let's get rid of them as quickly as possible,' he murmured before turning the ornate gold handle.

The woman who entered the room was stunning—the epitome of all that was chic. She was wearing a Chanel suit in a pale ivory, teamed with a coffee-coloured blouse. Her thick blonde hair was woven back from her oval face in a stylish plait that must have taken hours to achieve.

Drew spoke to her in French for a moment before bringing her further into the room to introduce her to Amanda.

Liliane Dassault's sharp brown eyes roved over Amanda assessingly. 'So, you are the designer who is ready to take Paris by storm,' she said in a honeyed French accent.

'That's right.' Drew placed a casual arm around her shoulders. 'Amanda is going to make a lot of the fashion houses sit up and take notice. Her work is quite simply brilliant.'

Amanda felt a warm glow spreading through her at the touch of his hand and his words of praise, even though she knew he was acting for the benefit of the article the woman would write.

'Shall we make ourselves more comfortable?' Drew said, steering them towards the easy chairs and settee.

They had just sat down when the photographer arrived, and he set up his camera and took a few photographs of her and Drew sitting next to each other on the settee as Liliane grilled them with a million and one questions.

Amanda found the next couple of hours arduous. It was easy enough talking about her training and the type of work she had been doing at Hunter's. It was when the questions started to get on to more personal ground that it became uncomfortable. Liliane seemed to be particularly interested in Drew's social life. She flirted outrageously with him, fluttering her dark lashes and sending him smouldering looks from sherry-brown eyes. Drew looked amused by it all. He fielded her questions easily, answering the personal questions without giving anything away. He made no reference to the fact that he was engaged, but hinted that there was someone special in his life. Amanda tried to ignore the wave of jealousy that washed over her at that.

As Liliane seemed to be on the verge of even more probing, Drew glanced at his watch. 'I'm afraid that's all we have time for,' he said on a note of regret. 'Amanda and I have some important work to attend to this afternoon.'

'Of course.' The Frenchwoman started to pack away her tape recorder and notebook. 'Perhaps we could just have a couple more photographs of you both outside?' She motioned her head towards the roof garden.

Drew nodded his assent and they all made their way outside into the sunshine. Liliane and the photographer prowled all over the garden searching for the best positions for the photographs. Drew and Amanda were left alone for a moment of brief respite.

'She's a little harder to get rid of than I envisaged,' Drew said in a low voice.

'I think she's taken a shine to you,' replied Amanda in a dry voice which barely concealed a note of resentment.

Drew grinned at her. 'Why, Amanda, you sound as if that bothers you.'

'Not in the slightest,' she retorted crossly. She was sure he was going to retaliate, but Liliane pre-empted him by calling out from around the corner, for them to join her.

When they did walk around, Amanda was surprised to see the Frenchwoman standing next to a large, gleaming helicopter.

'I didn't know that was there,' Amanda gasped in surprise. 'Whatever do you need it for?'

Drew grinned. 'It beats getting stuck in the Paris traffic.'

Liliane motioned impatiently for them to stand in front of the machine for a photograph, and the next few moments were taken up with the photographer giving them clipped directions as to how they should smile, how they should look at each other. At one point he asked Drew to hold her in his arms for a romantic picture and she pulled away abruptly. 'Is all this really necessary?' she asked sharply. 'Surely they've taken enough photographs now.'

'I was just starting to enjoy myself,' said Drew with a grin, but he turned to Liliane and brought the interview to an end.

The photographer left immediately, but the Frenchwoman lingered a while longer. As Drew walked with her to the door she turned and looked up at him, her lips curving in a provocative smile as she said something to him in French. Amanda didn't understand a word of what was said, but she could guess.

She sat down on the settee and tried to look unconcerned as the door closed behind the other woman and Drew turned towards her.

'Well, I'm glad that's finished with,' he said, loosening his tie and moving towards the drinks cabinet. 'Will you join me in a drink?'

Amanda shook her head. 'Was Liliane's invitation for dinner or bed?' she asked with a tight little smile. She knew that she should not have asked that, but somehow she just couldn't help herself.

Drew finished pouring his drink before looking at her. 'Dinner,' he answered easily. His eyes narrowed on her for a moment. 'For a woman who doesn't speak French, you don't do so badly at interpreting.'

She shrugged lightly. 'Sometimes a woman doesn't need words to put two and two together.' She would have liked to ask if he had accepted the invitation, but she had already overstepped the mark.

'I told her I had other plans,' he said, as if reading her mind. He smiled. 'I thought I'd better tell you, in case you added up wrong.'

'Well, it's really none of my business.' She got up and crossed towards the windows.

'In a way, it is,' he said softly, making her swing around to look questioningly at him. 'Well, my other plans included you. I thought we could go out for dinner and take in a few of the sights. What do you say?' He gave her a smile that did strange things to her pulse-rate.

'We shouldn't, there's so much work waiting for us in the office,' she said, while a little voice inside was clamouring for her to say, 'Yes, let's go.'

He glanced at his watch. 'The afternoon has practically gone. We may as well make the most of what's left of the day.' He tossed back the remainder of his drink. 'Let's be devils and skip work today,' he grinned. That smile of his was really infectious, and she found herself grinning back.

'Sounds good to me,' she said, not giving herself time to think too deeply about that feeling of elation that was flooding through her.

* * *

Amanda would never forget that afternoon. Paris was a vibrant, exciting city, and it seemed all the more so in Drew's company.

The horse-chestnut trees were in bloom, their delicate white blossoms giving a sweet perfume to the boulevards. The azaleas and flowering bulbs accented the fresh green of the grass and foliage.

They took the hotel's Mercedes Benz on a leisurely tour of the city, and then Drew asked the driver to drop them down by the banks of the River Seine. For a while they strolled along in companionable silence, broken only now and then as Drew pointed out a special place of interest.

A boat glided towards them over the blue water of the river and they stopped to watch it as it floated dreamily under one of the many bridges.

'That was one of the *bateaux mouches*.' Drew smiled down at Amanda. 'They cruise through the very heart of Paris and give some spectacular views.'

'I'd love a ride on one.' Her face glowed with excitement. 'Do you think we could?'

He smiled at her enthusiasm. 'I don't see why not.' He glanced at his watch. 'Although I warn you, they'll probably be packed with tourists and screaming children.'

'Well, as today I'm only a tourist myself, I won't object,' she said happily as they walked on. 'And besides, I love children.' She shot him a sideways glance. 'Don't you?'

'Yes.' He pulled her closer and rested an arm casually around her shoulders. 'But I think I'll probably have more patience with them when they're my own running wild.'

'Would you like children of your own?' she asked curiously.

'Well, that's something I have yet to discuss with my future wife.' He grinned down at her. 'But yes, I would like children.'

Amanda felt her heart growing cold as he spoke. It was the first time he had openly spoken about his marriage with Jordan. Suddenly she wished that she hadn't agreed to go out with him this afternoon. It was a mistake, she knew it was. Drew squeezed her arm gently. 'Here we are, Pont de l'Alma, and we're in luck. There's a riverboat waiting.' He guided her down towards the pier.

The boat was almost empty, and they had their pick of where to sit. 'I'm disappointed,' Amanda joked lightly as they sat alone on the top deck. 'Not one screaming child or tourist to be seen.'

'We'll have to come back when it's a little warmer and I'll arrange it,' Drew smiled. He put a protective arm around her as the boat pulled away from the pier. 'Anyway, I'm not complaining, I think I like just having you to distract me.'

She shivered slightly at the delicious sensations he stirred within her.

'You really should have a warmer coat on,' Drew said with concern. He opened his large overcoat and pulled her closer into the warmth of his body. 'Better?' he asked softly, and she nodded, feeling a little guilty at the fact that her shivers had not been from the cold. It felt so good being close to him, and she snuggled happily against his chest. He took the earphones that they had been handed when he paid. 'You don't need these. I'll be your guide today.'

The boat glided calmly down the Seine and Amanda gazed in wonder, from the warmth of Drew's arms, at the beautiful bridges and the impressive buildings which lined the river. Every now and then he pointed out a different place, telling her a little about them in a soft, deep voice close to her ear. Notre Dame, the most celebrated of Paris churches, loomed above them. High up on the balustrades and towers the famous gargoyles looked down, evoking visions of Quasimodo and medieval Paris.

Drew watched her delight in everything, enjoying her rapture. He pointed over at the huge block occupying nearly all of the Ile de la Cité. 'That's the Palais de Justice, which is now the municipal court of law. It was occupied in olden times by French kings, and before that by Roman governors.'

Amanda looked over at the ancient walls and pointed towers, which were awe-inspiring. Her hair fell to one side over her eyes as she moved her head to glance up at Drew, and he brushed it gently back for her. The action made her forget her surroundings and she found herself deeply aware of his closeness. She felt heat radiate through her entire body, and was painfully conscious of the restlessness he was stirring up within her.

She felt herself colour under the dark scrutiny of his eyes. Her lashes closed as his head moved down towards hers, and she trembled as she felt the featherlight touch of his lips on the coolness of her forehead and then her cheek. 'I'm glad we're friends again,' he murmured in a low voice. Her heart skipped a beat as the warmth of his lips captured hers in a fleeting hard kiss, but before she could respond to him he had moved away. 'You're missing the sights,' he said lightly.

Amanda, glancing at him from beneath her lashes, could read no expression on his face; he seemed undisturbed by the fierce sensual heat that burned as soon as their lips touched. To him that had just been a casual, friendly kiss, but to Amanda it was much more. She had longed for that kiss to deepen, her whole body seemed to be filled with an intense yearning.

They passed the Eiffel Tower and Amanda looked up at it through a haze of tears. I still love him, she thought, and the knowledge hit her like a physical blow, knocking the breath from her body, stunning her. I've always loved him, in spite of Jordan, in spite of everything. He was the one and only man she had ever wanted. She had been hiding from that fact for so long, it had been too painful to admit it even to herself. Perhaps that was why she had been so desperate to keep him at a distance, why she had used James like a wedge between them. Perhaps she had always known that if he came too close she wouldn't be able to pretend any more.

'Did you enjoy the trip?' Drew asked her as the boat pulled back into dock.

'Yes, very much, thank you.' She pulled away from the warmth of his arms, feeling awkward, embarrassed, almost frightened in case he should guess what had been going through her mind.

They walked through the Tuileries gardens, stopping for a moment to watch some little children beside the lake engrossed in manoeuvring their colourful miniature sail-boats with long poles from the shore, before strolling up the Rue de la Paix towards the Opéra, stopping occasionally to glance into the prestige jewellery shops. The precious stones shimmered alluringly under the lights.

'They're beautiful, don't you think?' Drew murmured close to her ear as they looked in the Cartier window.

'Stunning,' Amanda agreed. 'As are the prices.'

'I see they have your necklace in the window,' he said softly.

'My necklace?' She followed his eyes to the display in puzzlement, and then her lips curved in a soft smile as she saw the emerald necklace. Four beautiful stones encircled with diamonds, the setting perfectly matching the engagement ring that Drew had once placed on her finger.

'I always did say that emeralds were your stone; they match those sparkling eyes of yours.'

'You told me that the day we got engaged,' she said, and her voice held a wistful note.

'I remember.' He pulled her around to face him, but she couldn't look up at him, couldn't let him see the pain that was in her heart. What sort of engagement ring had he given Jordan? she wondered. A sapphire to match her blue eyes?

'Amanda, I...' he began, and his voice held a tinge of regret that made her pull away hastily. She didn't want him to say anything kind—that would be the last straw. She couldn't cope with that kind of humiliation. She was angry with herself for being such a fool. How could she still love a man who had been so flagrantly unfaithful to her? If she hadn't been with him this afternoon he would probably be sweet-talking the beautiful French girl who had interviewed them, or phoning Jordan to tell her how much he missed her. Drew was just a rat when it came to women, but God, even though she knew that, she still loved him.

'It's in the past, Drew,' she said quickly. 'Let's just leave it there.'

CHAPTER NINE

THE sky darkened ominously and Drew looked upwards, swearing under his breath. 'It's going to rain. Come on, let's get out of here.' They walked on in silence, then the rain started to fall heavily, making the cobblestoned streets glow and reflect the colourful raincoats and umbrellas that passers-by suddenly produced.

'There's a good restaurant up here. If we hurry, we might escape getting drenched.' Drew started to lengthen his strides and Amanda had to practically run to keep up with him.

When at last he came to a standstill under a bright red awning she almost fell against him. His hands reached out automatically to steady her. 'Are you all right?' He looked down at her, his face very close.

She nodded and made to move away from him, but he held her near. 'Do you love James Reece?' he asked her suddenly, his voice low. She could feel his body tensing as he waited for her to answer.

There were dark shadows in her eyes as she looked upwards. 'Sometimes I don't think people know the meaning of that word,' she whispered. 'They seem to use it like some magic phrase to gain someone's affections and then, when they've had their fun, it's on to the next conquest.'

'So you've decided to play it safe and marry someone you don't love.' He frowned. 'That's the guaranteed road to unhappiness. You're a warm, passionate woman. You shouldn't lock your heart away and deny yourself the joys and rewards of loving.'

'The joy can fade very quickly into tears and heartaches,' she said in an undertone.

He nodded. 'Yes, it can, but nothing on this earth that's worth while comes easily.' He tipped her chin gently upwards, and there was a burning flame in his eyes as he looked at her delicate oval face. 'The secret is to find the right partner, the right combination. Don't give up on love completely.'

The door of the restaurant opened behind them and some people came out. Drew smiled at her. 'Let's go and have something to eat.'

The restaurant was exclusive and it was very busy. For a moment Amanda wondered if they would be able to get a table. The way the head waiter fussed over Drew soon dispelled that thought. The patronage of Drew Sheldon was clearly an honour. In a matter of minutes they were seated at the best table.

'You always get what you want, don't you, Drew?' she said in a low voice as she glanced around. They were in a private alcove, stained-glass windows in the gothic dark partitions. Candlelight gleamed over the silver on the table.

'Usually.' He looked up from his study of the menu. 'What would you like to drink?'

'A glass of wine, please.'

He raised his head the merest fraction and immediately the head waiter was beside them. Drew gave their order in rapid French and then turned towards her. 'Have you decided what you would like to eat?'

Amanda glanced down at the menu and couldn't understand one word of it.

'Would you like me to order for you?' he asked.

'No!' The word came out with forceful emphasis. She knew if she started to let him take her over she would be on dangerous ground. She must not start to depend on him for anything—no matter how small. If she did she would be completely devastated when he went out of her life again. God knew, it was going to be hard enough now that she realised how much she felt for him.

'I'm quite capable of deciding for myself, thank you,' she said coolly.

'Always so independent,' he mocked lightly. She ignored him and pointed decisively at the list of starters and main courses. 'I'll have those, please.'

He laughed. 'As you wish.' And he gave the order to the waiter who was hovering patiently. 'You do know what you ordered, I take it?' he asked as the waiter left.

'This may come as a surprise to you, Drew, but I am able to take care of myself,' she prevaricated.

'So I see.' His dark eyes glittered with humour. 'I must admit your choice surprises me. I didn't think you would have gone for that sort of thing. Mind you, I didn't think you would have gone for James either, so I'm obviously no judge of your tastes.'

Amanda frowned, wondering what she had ordered, but she was determined not to ask him. His next words made her eyes widen with horror.

'You've obviously got a liking for toads,' he said drily.

'All right, just exactly what have I ordered?' Against all her convictions, she just had to ask him.

'I thought you knew.' His lips twitched irritatingly. 'I would never have ordered frogs' legs and fresh eels grilled in lemon and white wine sauce for you. Your tastes have become very adventurous since we last dined together.'

'You're joking, I didn't really order that, did I?' she floundered, absolutely horrified at the prospect of that meal being placed in front of her. 'You'll have to change that order, Drew,' she suddenly burst out. 'I can't possibly eat that!'

He laughed; it was a contagious sound and she felt herself relax, a humorous smile curve her lips. 'I'm warning you, Drew, I won't be able to look at that food, let alone eat it,' she told him, trying to remain stern.

He laughed again. 'Amanda, you're priceless. You make such a fuss about being independent and you're so fiercely stubborn, yet when it comes down to it you're as vulnerable as a child.'

'Well, I'm glad you find me so amusing,' she answered stiffly. 'If you're going to continue making fun of me, and if you let that waiter bring that—that reptile, I'm going back to the hotel right now.'

Drew's eyes sparkled and he looked as if he was having difficulty restraining himself from laughing again. 'For your information, I changed your order when I gave it to the waiter. Though it would serve you right if I hadn't.' He leaned back in his chair, his mouth curved in a lop-sided grin. 'I'd forgotten what an entertaining dinner companion you are.'

'Well, you haven't given me a chance to forget how irritating you are,' she murmured.

He smiled, unperturbed. 'Do you remember that meal we had together in the Lake District, the first day we met?'

She nodded and looked away from his dark eyes. She would never forget that special time, it was indelibly printed in her memory for all time.

'You told me there were no men in your life who were important to you,' he said gently.

'So I did.' She turned her eyes directly on him now, remembering the feelings that had accompanied that statement. She had wanted him with all her heart. As she looked at him now, so devastatingly attractive, the same overwhelming feeling rushed through her.

'Were you telling the truth, or was James important even then?' he asked, his face expressionless.

Her eyes veered away again at the direct question. 'James wasn't important then,' she had to answer honestly, her voice husky with emotion.

The waiter arrived with their first course and there was silence as he served them.

'So your relationship with James didn't develop until after we got engaged?' he continued as soon as the waiter left them.

She reached for her wineglass. 'I don't want to discuss my relationship with James,' she told him coolly. 'It's none of your business.'

'I think it is. I think I have a right to know. After all, you did break our engagement for him.' His face was etched with stern lines.

'You have no rights,' she breathed in protest, suddenly angry. 'Tell me, Drew, while we were engaged, were all your business trips as cosy as this?' She indicated the intimate table, the romantic restaurant, with an expressive sweep of one delicate hand. 'Or is this reserved for business associates who are a little more stubborn when it comes to falling into bed with you?' she finished with bitter contempt.

'I can't think of any business associates I would want to fall into bed with,' he said calmly, and picked up his wineglass. 'Present company excluded.'

Amanda sent him a fulminating glare from ice-green eyes. What about Jordan Lee? she wanted to scream, but the words wouldn't form in her mouth. She couldn't expose her feelings to him—her hurt and her pain. To do so would only be to feed his male ego and vanity. She would never allow him to know how deeply he had hurt her. Her nails dug deep into the palms of her hand as they rested on the table. No doubt he would be interested in having a casual fling with her, or, if she hadn't agreed to this outing, he would be propositioning the beautiful Liliane who had interviewed them earlier. Drew was just a compulsive womaniser. 'Well, you can just forget about me, because I'm not interested or available.'

'If you say so.' His eyes rested thoughtfully on her hands as they twisted nervously. She looked down at the untouched food in front of her. Usually fresh oysters poached in a white wine sauce was one of her favourite starters, but she just couldn't bring herself to eat it.

'Don't you like what I ordered for you?' Drew asked, and there was a concerned note in his voice.

'It's lovely, thank you.' She toyed with the food, trying to feign some interest in it.

'Better than the eels, I assure you.' He tried to raise a smile.

The generous curve of her lips gave a somewhat shaky smile, and her golden-green eyes had a sad, faraway look for a moment before the thick sweep of her lashes fluttered down to conceal them.

The waiter arrived with their main course—*feuilleté* of lamb with truffles. Amanda reached for her wine and then thought better of it. She didn't dare drink on an empty stomach, she needed to keep all her wits about her.

'So, if you don't love James, why do you need him?' Drew asked, his eyes fixed unwaveringly on her.

'I don't need him,' she answered heatedly, without really thinking. 'I don't need anyone,' she added, aware that a puzzled look had crossed his face.

'You have a very cynical, wary view of human relationships.' Drew took a drink of his wine and put it down before continuing, 'I noticed that wariness when I was first dating you; it was almost as if you were testing me out sometimes.'

'Maybe I was,' she agreed. 'After all, your reputation with women did precede you.' And I was right to be wary, she thought. Maybe if I'd listened to intuition I would never have allowed myself to get in so deep with him in the first place.

'What reputation?' he asked, his eyes narrowing.

'Look, I've told you, I don't want to talk about this,' she reiterated.

'You don't love James, you don't need him, yet you're going to marry him,' Drew continued as if she hadn't spoken. He shook his head. 'Amanda, I just can't understand you.'

'Well, you don't need to understand, it's nothing to do with you.' She pushed back her hair with a nervous hand. 'I'm not a clinging-vine type of female, I'm a career girl. I don't need any man.'

'Now you're sounding like some hard-line Women's Libber, and I know deep down that's not your style.'

'You don't know anything about my style.' Her eyes blazed. 'I watched my parents' marriage disintegrate because my father had no time for my mother. His first love in life was his business, and my mother wasn't able to cope with that. She needed him, but he was never there for her, so don't talk to me about needing someone.' She bit her lip and glanced away, mortified at her outburst. 'That sounds as if I'm blaming my father for their divorce, and I don't,' she said quietly and honestly. 'All I'm saying is that needing someone isn't such a good idea, you've got to be self-sufficient.'

'Even the most self-sufficient people need someone special in their lives, Amanda,' he said gently. 'It's a fundamental human instinct. All right, your parents got it wrong.' He spread his hands. 'It happens, but you can't allow their experiences to cloud your view of things. Relationships are delicate things, they need to be nurtured, worked at. Don't let one bitter experience ruin your life.'

Two bitter experiences, she thought with a wry twist of her lips. There was silence for a moment, then Drew leaned forward. 'Did you ever compare our relationship with your parents' when we were engaged?' he asked in a low voice. 'Was that why you suddenly turned to James? Did you think a relationship with him would be safer?'

'There were certain similarities,' she admitted grudgingly. 'The broken dates, the weeks when I was never sure where you were. But my father never...' She stopped suddenly, aware that she was betraying her feelings, leaving herself open to him. She had been going to say that her father had never been unfaithful, but she wasn't supposed to care about Drew's infidelity; that was all in the past and she must never reveal how much he had hurt her. Her lashes fluttered down. 'But that's irrelevant. I found someone who was kind and...'

'Kind!' Drew exploded angrily. 'You broke our engagement because James was kind? Is that what you're trying to tell me?'

'I'm trying to tell you that it's none of your business,' she said as calmly as she could. 'We've been getting on quite well since we arrived in Paris, Drew; don't spoil things.' She put her cutlery down, although she had barely touched her meal. 'It's getting late, Drew, don't you think we should go?'

Somewhat to her surprise, he immediately agreed and signalled for the waiter. He hadn't eaten very much either, she realised as she watched their plates being removed. He looked tired as well, she noticed with a sudden tug at her heartstrings.

'Would you like some coffee before we leave?' he asked her politely, and she shook her head.

'Perhaps when we get back to the hotel.'

When they did arrive back at the Sheldon, Drew was immediately detained by the hotel's manager. So Amanda went up alone to the apartment.

Mechanically she made herself coffee in the ultramodern kitchen and then brought it through into the lounge. For a while she sat drinking it, staring into the flames of the fire which burnt brightly in the elegant fireplace. She shouldn't feel so shocked by the realisation that she still loved Drew, it should have been obvious to her. Why else should she feel so deeply every time he looked at her, every time he kissed her? Her mouth twisted ruefully. She had always known that Drew was the reason she hadn't been interested in any other man. It was obvious that he had still been in her blood—in her heart. She jumped nervously at some sound outside in the corridor, thinking it might be Drew. The noise passed and she relaxed again as she finished her coffee and moved to the sanctuary of her own room.

She needed some time on her own; she couldn't face Drew again until her emotions were tightly under control.

Amanda could not sleep again that night. She tossed and turned, her mind and her body burning with the knowledge of her love for Drew. Restlessly she got out of her bed and moved to open the glass doors to the roof garden. The cool breeze against her fevered skin was sheer bliss, and on impulse she stepped outside.

The grass was cold under her bare feet, the breeze ruffled the silk of her long white nightdress and lifted her hair back from her hot skin. She walked across towards the parapet and leaned against it as she looked out over Paris. It glittered, bright and alive with lights. Even though it was four a.m. the city was awake and alive. She could almost feel its pulse beating through the cold stone wall she was leaning against. She took a deep breath of the spring air and looked up at the sky, its velvet darkness lit with the golden glow of the city. Everything seemed to radiate with light and energy, so that when she turned to look back at the garden it seemed like a tranquil haven in the midst of all that heat and excitement.

The only light in the garden came from the pool. It was lit from beneath, making the water shimmer a deep turquoise colour. Amanda moved gracefully towards it, drawn by the serenity of the blue, motionless water, and on impulse she bent and trailed her hand through its calm surface. It felt surprisingly warm; it must be constantly kept heated, she thought. Suddenly she was filled with an overwhelming urge to slip into the soft turquoise water. She only hesitated a moment. There was no one about, the roof was completely private and Drew would have been asleep for hours now. With a quick glance around the darkened garden she undid the top buttons of her nightdress and let it slither to the ground before lowering her slim body into the silky warmth of the water.

It felt so good gliding through the water that she swam length after length, needing the exercise to release all the pent-up tension that had built up over the last few days. She was a strong, graceful swimmer, cutting through the water with smooth ease, her hair fanning out around her, dark against the blue of the water. She twisted and dived underwater, staying there until she reached the end of the pool. When she surfaced she was blinded by her hair and water, and for a moment she clung to the edge, blinking until the blurred shadows of the garden started to come back into focus. A sudden movement brought all her senses sharply back into distinct clarity. Her breath froze in a sudden gasp as she saw Drew sitting lazily on one of the softly padded chairs next to the pool.

'How—how long have you been sitting there?' she gulped nervously, clinging desperately to the side of the pool in order to hide her naked body from him.

'Long enough,' he smiled.

A slow flush of humiliated heat washed over her. He would have been able to see her body clearly in the brightly lit pool.

'Why aren't you in bed?' She suddenly noticed that he was wearing the same grey suit he had been wearing earlier.

'I've been working. What's your excuse?' He picked up a glass from the table beside him and took a sip of the golden liquid as if sitting watching her bathing nude was just a regular, everyday occurrence.

'I—I couldn't sleep.' She frantically cast her eyes about for her nightdress and was horrified to see it at the other end of the pool. 'Drew—I—I don't have any clothes on.' She gulped back an overwhelming urge to scream at him to get lost.

'So I noticed.'

She cringed at the open admiration in his voice. 'Do—do you think you could pass me a towel or something?' she asked in a voice that trembled alarmingly.

He grinned and reached around the back of his chair. 'I brought one of my towelling robes out for you,' he said, holding it up. 'You'd better hurry and get out of there, or you'll catch cold. It's really too early in the year for bathing out here.'

Yes, now that she had stopped swimming she was starting to shiver. 'Will you pass me the robe, please?' She held out one long, slim arm pleadingly towards him.

He stood up and she immediately shrank back as close to the edge as possible. 'Come on, then.' She could hear the teasing note in his voice as he held the robe.

'Just throw it down to me,' she said angrily through clenched teeth.

His eyebrows lifted mockingly. 'What, and get it all wet?'

'Drew!' Her voice was sharp with anger. 'If you don't give me that robe I'll—I'll——' She floundered to a halt, unable to think of anything bad enough to do to him.

'Yes, what will you do?' He sounded as if he was enjoying himself, and her blood boiled.

'Drew, so help me, you're going to be sorry if you don't give me that damn robe and disappear!' She trembled as much with cold as fury.

'I don't know why you're suddenly acting so prudish,' he drawled. 'After all, it's not as if I haven't seen that beautiful body of yours before.'

Amanda's face drained of all colour. 'God, I hate you!'

'I told you before about that,' he said drily. 'You don't hate me, Amanda. Maybe you're a little afraid of me, but you certainly don't hate me.'

'Well, I'm not afraid of you, that's for sure,' she denied virulently.

'No?' One eyebrow rose mockingly. 'Then why are you hiding down there, shivering?' He crouched down so that his face was alarmingly close to hers. 'I'll tell you what, we'll make a deal.' His eyes raked over her pale, upturned face glistening with tiny drops of water, noticing the nervous way she caught her bottom lip in pearly white teeth. 'I'll give you the robe if you tell me exactly why you broke our engagement and exactly what your feelings for James are,' he said quietly.

'Go to hell!' Her eyes widened with fury. 'It's none of your damn business!'

He shrugged and made to move away from her with the robe. She snatched out in an attempt to pull it away from him, but he moved too fast for her. 'Every time you refuse I'm going to move a step away from you and you'll have further to walk to get your robe,' he told her calmly.

'You . . .' Unspeakable adjectives flew to her lips, but she stemmed them in time. Drew was enjoying himself, playing games with her—well, two could play at that game. 'All right, you win. Give me the robe and we'll talk.'

He shook his head. 'Oh, no, talk first, then I hand you the wrap.'

'Drew, please, I'm freezing.' Amanda shivered violently. 'If you let me out of here I promise to give you what you're asking for.' She let out her breath in a relieved sigh as he threw the robe down on the concrete beside her and turned his back. She climbed quickly out of the pool and pulled it on. It was far too large for her and hung from her slender frame, but the soft warmth it gave her chilled body was heaven.

'Well?' He turned to look at her and she shivered, brushing her wet hair back from her face with an unsteady hand. 'Drew, I'm so cold,' she murmured softly. She watched him from under her dark eyelashes as he moved across towards her.

'Come on, we'd better get you inside and give you a brandy.' He placed a concerned hand on her shoulder and she looked up at him through seductive green-gold eyes.

'Just hold me for a moment—will you, Drew?' she asked him quietly. She could see the surprise in his face

as she reached her slim arms up and around his broad
shoulders. She flicked her eyes downwards momentarily
to gauge how close to the edge of the pool he was
standing. Not close enough, she determined as she moved
around him slightly to get a better position.

'Drew.' She whispered his name throatily as she stood
on tiptoe, her lips inches from his. She could feel his
cool breath fanning against her skin, feel her nerves
prickle at the back of her neck. She wanted to kiss him,
she was so close that the desire was devastating. He made
no move to close that small gap between them, standing
still, almost as if he was waiting for the touch of her lips
with bated breath. For a moment there was a sweet
silence as they stood close, then Drew gave a small groan
as he bent his head to take possession of her lips.

That small sound deep in his throat was enough to
bring Amanda back to her senses, and before he could
wrap his arms around her she placed her hands flat
against his chest and pushed with all her strength,
knowing the pool was directly behind him.

'Why, you...' The rest of his words were lost as he
crashed down into the turquoise-blue water. Amanda
stood with her hands on her hips, the gleam of a smile
on her slightly parted lips.

'You asked for that,' she told him as he surfaced. But
her feeling of triumph was short-lived as she saw the
dark fury on his face. Suddenly she didn't think it was
a good idea to gloat and, terrified, she turned and fled
through the lounge doors towards the safety of her room.

She closed her door with a resounding slam and turned
the key, leaning her ear against the solid wood, anxious
to hear if he was following her. The apartment was
deathly silent; all she could hear was the heavy thud of
her frightened heartbeat. God, why ever had she done
that? she wondered frantically. If Drew got his hands
on her he would probably shake the life out of her. That
suit he had been wearing must have cost a fortune and
she had most probably ruined it.

She clenched her hands into tight fists and strained to hear what he was doing. Where was he? The silence was unbearable.

'Listening for something?' The deep voice in the darkness of her room sent her spinning around in shock. Drew was standing inside the french doors, leaning indolently against their frame. For a moment she was so frightened she thought she was going to faint—she had completely forgotten about those doors!

'You shouldn't have done that, Amanda.' She couldn't see the expression on his face—his whole body was in dark shadow—but she could hear the soft menace in his voice and it was enough to make her scrabble wildly for the doorkey. Her hands were trembling so much that she could hardly turn it, and as she cast a glance back at him she saw he was coming closer and knew there was no way she was going to escape him!

'Don't you dare touch me!' she warned in a high, unsteady voice, but he kept coming closer and closer. He towered over her, dark and powerful. 'Drew, please...' Her voice changed to a pleading tone.

He stopped, his body only inches from hers, and leaned one hand heavily on the door behind her. 'Now, where were we?' His voice was deep and calm, but there was an undertone which sent warning bells ringing through her body. She licked her lips nervously.

'Ah, yes.' One hand brought her chin up firmly so that she was forced to look up at him, then it trailed dangerously down her neckline to where her robe was slightly parted. Deliberately he ran his hand further down, trailing it softly through the sensitive valley of her breasts and down to her waist. It stopped there for a moment, his hand cool against her burning skin.

She was trembling uncontrollably, her eyes locked with his. She didn't dare speak. His hands moved, and flagrantly he untied the belt of her robe so that it fell away from her slender frame in a crumpled heap at their feet.

She stood naked in front of him and her body burned as his eyes moved from her face in a deliberately intimate perusal.

'No!' The word was strangled in her throat; even as she was saying it she could feel her body responding to him. Her breasts felt suddenly heavy, aching for his touch. Then she could feel the soft, wet fabric of his suit pressed against them as he gathered her close. His hand, resting in the hollow of her back, felt like a burning brand.

She gave a small gasp as his lips touched her neck and then moved upwards to her ear. She tried to keep her arms stiffly at her sides, but they wanted to wind around him. She wanted to touch him, kiss him. The longing was an unbearable pain deep inside her.

'Now I'm going to show you what happens to tormenting, unscrupulous little witches.' His voice was a low growl against her skin, making her shiver, but this time it was with desire, not fear. Raw with longing, she pressed closer as his lips came down on hers in a long kiss of savage passion. His skin was rough against the smooth velvet softness of hers and she raised her hand to trace it wonderingly along the rugged line of his jaw. She loved the familiar feel of him—wanted him so much.

He scooped her up in strong arms and carried her to the bed, laying her down with infinite care. For a moment he stood looking down at her, then he loosened his tie to throw it to the floor, his jacket and then his shirt following closely.

Amanda swallowed hard as she looked up at his powerful build. The moonlight slanted through the window, gleaming over his raven-black hair. He looked like a Greek god in that strange half-light. She knew every inch of his body intimately, had ached for it night after night. Hungered for his lovemaking, his tender kisses. Now he was going to take her out of anger; he didn't love her and yet she still wanted him.

Her eyes were a brilliant gold, filled with unshed tears. He hesitated, his hand on the buckle of his trousers. 'Amanda?'

She couldn't answer him; if she spoke she would break down and sob her heart out.

'Amanda, for God's sake don't look at me like that.' He sat down on the edge of the bed beside her, his rage dissolving at the agony in her eyes. 'You know I won't force you. I've never forced a woman in my life, I don't intend to start now.' His face was dark with some inner emotion she couldn't quite make out. 'You want me. I know you do.'

'It would be just casual—I don't want——' Her voice was broken, incoherent with emotion.

He watched a tear trickle down her pale face. 'God, Amanda, I don't want to hurt you.' He reached out a hand to wipe her tears and she flinched visibly away. If he touched her she would lose all self-control. She wanted him so much, wanted him to take her into his arms and love her.

He stared down at her, grim-faced. 'So you really do love the guy!' He got up from the bed and bent to retrieve his clothing. He didn't even look up at her again but moved towards the door. 'Don't worry, Amanda, I won't bother you again.'

As soon as the door closed behind him she turned her face into the silk pillows and wept tears of bitter anguish.

CHAPTER TEN

CLAUDE was handing her masses of paper, neatly dated, neatly clipped together, beautifully typed. None of them seemed to be making much sense. The words kept jiggling about on the pages. Amanda suddenly felt a huge wave of tiredness washing over her; she felt almost faint with it, her stomach turning over in protest. It was all the sleepless nights, she supposed. She hadn't slept properly in weeks, ever since that incident with Drew in her bedroom. She was pushing herself very hard to work the long hours that were necessary to plan a major fashion show.

'Before we start, could I have a drink of water?' She looked up at the dark face of her assistant and it seemed to blur for a moment.

As Claude came back with a goblet, she forced herself to pay attention to the lists in front of her, add up figures, read closely. As she read she relaxed a little. She had always been able to lose herself in ideas, spin out of a depression with new thoughts. She began to feel peace moving over her, smoothing out the worried frown on her forehead. She could almost forget the detached coolness in Drew's voice when he spoke to her, the indifference in his eyes when he looked at her.

Claude talked to her as she read, pulling out papers, changing the order of the pages she held, but she didn't allow him to distract her. The fashion show was well under way, the dates for the big Press show were set, the all-important buyers had accepted their invitations, the shipments were due. Now models had to be hired, music arranged and a commentator set.

'Have you seen the article about you in *Jours de France*?' Claude asked suddenly. 'They sent it over to us this morning.'

Amanda shook her head and watched as he rifled through the papers on Drew's desk, looking for the magazine. Drew had left the office hours ago. He hadn't mentioned where he was going, probably sorting out some problem in the hotel. Amanda never stopped marvelling at the way Drew coped with all the pressure he was under. Not only was he dealing with the fashion show and new boutique, but he was constantly deluged with correspondence from his hotels in every corner of the globe. It wasn't really surprising that he had been in a black mood just recently. His staff's mistakes and trivial problems had been dealt with with his usual patience, but no one had dared to push him too far, otherwise sparks would fly. Drew wasn't in any mood to tolerate nonsense.

'It's a good photograph, don't you think?'

Amanda glanced down and focused on the page Claude had opened in front of her. Yes, it was a good photograph. It was the one that had been taken beside the helicopter, she encircled in Drew's arms, looking up at him. He looked powerful and handsome, and her auburn hair was tossed back as she gazed up at him in contemplation. To Amanda, her love for him seemed to shine through the picture; it was obvious, from the bright, vivacious look on her face to the lines of her body. She glanced down at the article underneath, but couldn't understand one word. 'What does she say about us?' She glanced questioningly up at Claude.

He grinned. 'It's all very complimentary, especially about Drew; but I think perhaps the beautiful Liliane Dassault may be biased. She seems to have taken a—how do you say?' He hesitated for a moment. 'Ah, yes, a desire for him.' He nodded. 'She has phoned the hotel on quite a few occasions.'

'Has she?' Amanda said in dull interest. She didn't really want to hear this. She closed the magazine with a snap.

Claude went on undeterred. 'But Monsieur Sheldon is unimpressed, he has left strict instructions that he is not available when she phones.'

'Really?' Amanda's eyebrows rose, but before she had time to think about that the door of the office opened and Drew came in.

'What's the latest update on the accepted invitations for the show?' he demanded, making Claude jump to find the relevant figures.

Amanda closed the magazine in front of her and turned her attention back to the work she had been studying. Her nerves were jangling again at his presence in the room and she didn't look up.

The telephone's shrill ring broke the silence in the room and Claude snapped it up from Drew's desk. 'It's for you,' he told Amanda. 'A gentleman.'

'Oh!' Surprised, Amanda reached for the phone beside her. Her father's voice brought the first bright smile to her face in weeks.

'Hello, this is a lovely surprise.' Her eyes sparkled with happiness and lifted up from the pages of her work, only to collide with Drew's disapproving dark eyes. 'Yes, I'm fine, how are you?' she went on, trying to ignore the furious glare she was receiving from across the room. Drew might not agree with her receiving personal calls, but this was the first time she had spoken to her father in quite some time and she wasn't about to cut her conversation short just because she was displeasing him. 'Things are going very well here,' she assured him, and then gave a sad little smile as he asked if the business was missing him. 'Of course, things just aren't the same without you, and I miss you terribly.'

'Amanda, we have work to do,' Drew growled suddenly across to her. She disregarded him completely and went on to tell her father how the preparations for the fashion show were going, something she knew he would be interested in.

'I've sent you a letter, telling you all about it,' she finished, and laughed when her father said he had received it but wanted to hear about it anyway.

'Well, I'll have to go now,' she said, looking over and catching the full hostile stare from Drew.

When the conversation ended she put the receiver down and glared at him. 'Happy now?'

'I think I will get someone to send us some coffee,' Claude interjected quickly, as if sensing the atmosphere in the office, and moved quickly to the door.

'I don't pay you to have long conversations with your boyfriend,' Drew said caustically.

'That was hardly what I would call a long conversation,' Amanda snapped back heatedly. 'And that wasn't a boyfriend, it was my father.'

'I see.' Drew raked a hand through his dark hair. 'I'm sorry, Amanda. I think I'm just a little on edge lately,' he said. 'Have you heard anything of Reece lately?' he continued before she had time to reply.

She looked up, surprised at the unexpectedly personal question after weeks of his detachment.

'No, I haven't. I expect he's still lapping up the sun in Bermuda.'

'Yes.' Drew's tone was dry. 'But they do have phones there, he could ring you.'

Amanda shrugged; how could she tell him she wasn't interested or bothered whether James rang or not? 'He's probably far too busy to talk to me; he takes his work very seriously.'

'That's something you both seem to have in common,' Drew remarked lightly.

She nodded; yes, their work had been the only thing they had in common, all their conversation had centred on it. They had both been totally dedicated to their chosen careers. That enthusiasm had formed the basis of their friendship—but it would never have been enough to form any deeper feelings than that.

'I was wondering about photographers for the show,' he went on smoothly. 'Reece should be finished in Bermuda soon. Perhaps we should get him to come over and cover it.'

'If you like.' She tried to keep the flat, uninterested note out of her voice without much success.

'I'll get on to it, then,' he said, still watching her closely, a puzzled light in his eyes.

'Yes.' She flicked through the papers in front of her. 'I'm having difficulty deciding which models we should use for the show. It's hard to tell just looking at the girls' portfolios. It takes a very special model for runway work.'

'Have you drawn up a shortlist of the girls you think might be suitable?' His voice was businesslike and practical again.

'Yes, I've marked them on the files.' Amanda's red-gold hair gleamed in the lamplight of her desk as she bent forward to select the relevant file.

'Well, if you give them to me, I'll ring the agency and get them to send the girls over.' Drew got up from his desk and crossed the room to stand beside her. Ridiculously, that closeness made her hands tremble slightly and, knowing that nothing escaped his sharp eyes, she felt even more flustered. 'They're in here somewhere.' She flicked through the pages, her nervous eyes unable to find the names she knew were there.

'Amanda.' His large hands reached out and covered hers. 'Stop for a moment.'

Startled, she glanced up and he crouched down beside her, so that their faces were level. 'Do you want to talk about it?' he asked gently.

'Talk about what?' she asked, perplexed, her heart thudding wildly at the pressure of his hand over hers.

'The unhappy, troubled shadows in those beautiful eyes of yours. The translucent paleness of your skin.

Something is bothering you, Amanda; if you tell me what it is, maybe I can help.'

She gave a trembling half-smile. What would he say if she told him that he was the reason for her unhappy countenance? That she loved him with all her heart? He would probably find that very amusing. 'Why the sudden concern?' She pulled her hand away from his. 'You've hardly spoken two words to me over the last few weeks.'

'Well, that was the way you wanted it, wasn't it?' he demanded sharply.

'No.' The word just slipped out unchecked. His eyes moved swiftly over her face, for a second open and vulnerable before her eyelashes closed and she apologised, her cool, efficient mask back in place. 'You're quite right, that is how I want it.'

The door of the office opened before Drew could answer and Claude came in, a harassed expression on his young face. 'Sorry I was so long, Marion detained me. There is a discrepancy over the seating plans for the fashion show.' He looked ruefully over at his boss. 'Did you want the first three rows for the top fashion magazines or the first four?'

Drew straightened and raked a firm hand through his dark hair. 'Don't worry about it, Claude, I'm going up there now, so I'll sort it out.' He looked back at Amanda. 'You finish early for once and go and have dinner in the restaurant.'

She shook her head. 'I have far too much to do.'

'Sorry, Amanda, but I'm not going to allow you to work any more this evening.' He leaned over her and decisively switched off the powerful lamp on her desk. 'You looked washed out, you need some time to relax.'

'Why don't we all have dinner in the restaurant tonight?' Claude suddenly interrupted them. 'Things are running to schedule and it would do us all good to relax together for an hour or two.'

Drew hesitated momentarily and then nodded. 'Yes, I think you're right. Phone upstairs, will you, Claude, and make sure there's a table secured for us?' His dark eyes rested directly on Amanda. 'Does eight o'clock suit you?'

She nodded, the prospect of dining with him, no matter how many other people were present, bringing a sparkle back into her eyes.

The evening dress Amanda chose to wear was of white silk, long and clinging. It was almost the exact replica of the dress she had worn when she was modelling, the day she had first met Drew. She tried to tell herself that she was wearing it because it was the most suitable dress for the elaborate dining-room where royalty had rubbed shoulders with the world's most famous film stars. But deep down she knew that wasn't the only reason. She wanted to look good for Drew.

She wore no jewellery, leaving her perfectly shaped shoulders and neckline deliberately bare. Her hair was swept to one side and fell in burnished copper waves over her soft skin. The effect was blatantly erotic, yet Amanda had that vulnerable, untouched aura of true classical beauty.

As she approached the dining-room she could hear the rise and fall of voices, various languages, French, Italian, English and Spanish, contrasting and blending. Then the huge golden doors were opened for her and for a moment she was bedazzled by the crystal chandeliers glimmering over diamonds and rubies that adorned the many elegant women in the room.

'Ah, Mademoiselle Hunter!' The head waiter came over to her, surprising her by his use of her name. In a hotel filled with people it was an incredible accomplishment that he should know her. 'If you would like to follow me, your party is waiting for you.'

Amanda nodded and followed him across the enormous room, through the sea of fashionable dinner-jacketed men and women in Givenchys and Diors. Then she could see Drew's powerful figure, feel his eyes on her as she walked towards him. For an instant she thought she saw desire in the depths of his eyes as he observed the way the dress accentuated the perfect curves of her body. For one treasured moment they were in their own private world.

Then she reached the table and all the men were standing politely to welcome her.

'You look wonderful, *chérie*,' Claude breathed in admiration.

'Thank you.' She smiled around at the men who were all looking very elegant in their evening suits. They had all worked closely together organising various aspects of the forthcoming fashion show, and she felt perfectly at ease in their company. Drew stood slightly apart, easily towering over the other men; he looked dynamic. His dark hair gleamed in the soft light, his shoulders broad and powerful in the dark jacket. He seemed to overshadow every other man in the room. His firm mouth curved in a lopsided smile as he held out the chair next to him.

That smile did strange things to her heartbeat and made her hands tighten alarmingly on the delicate white sequined evening-bag she was carrying.

'Come and sit next to me,' he invited smoothly.

She moved to comply, and as everyone settled back into their chairs she looked around. 'Where's Marion?' she asked, more to cover her state of nervous excitement at the light touch of Drew's hand as he guided her into her chair.

'Making a few last-minute phone calls to the model agency for Drew,' Claude informed her easily.

She nodded. Marion was very good at her job; she had studied fashion at one of the leading Paris colleges. Amanda had found her help invaluable over the last few weeks.

A waiter handed her a menu and she was relieved to see it was in English. Drew turned and caught the look in her eye and grinned. 'That's especially for you, so that you don't order the eels.'

She met his gaze with a mischievous sparkle in her eyes. 'Actually, I think I'm feeling rather adventurous this evening.'

'Really?' One eyebrow rose and he leaned closer. 'Have you any idea what you're doing to my blood-pressure, saying things like that and looking so desirable?' His low, teasing voice had warm undercurrents that sent shivers running through her. She was saved from having to make a reply by Marion's arrival.

'I am sorry I am a little late,' she said in her delightful broken English. As the men started to rise she waved them down with an expressive sweep of her hands. 'No, no, please don't get up.' Quickly she sat down opposite Amanda, between Claude and Françoise.

'You look beautiful, Amanda,' she said candidly.

'Thank you, so do you,' answered Amanda warmly. The French girl did indeed look very lovely. She was wearing a chic blue-grey satin dress which matched the colour of her eyes perfectly and set off her sleek, dark hair to perfection.

'Did you sort things out with the agency?' Drew asked her.

'Yes, they'll send fifteen girls over tomorrow.'

'Good.' Drew smiled, satisfied with that. He signalled to the waiter and two arrived immediately, carrying silver ice-buckets and champagne.

'Are we celebrating already?' Amanda smiled.

'But of course.' Drew made sure everyone's glass was filled with the Moët et Chandon before raising his own. 'Here's to our talented designer and a very successful collection.'

Everyone smiled and lifted the elegant crystal glasses in salute towards her. Then the conversation became animated as they discussed different ideas for the show.

Amanda enjoyed that evening more than she could ever say. It wasn't just the superlative food or exciting exchange of ideas. It was Drew's presence next to her: the chivalrous way he paid attention to her, the quietly voiced comments that were for her ears only. Her cheeks were flushed with a warm glow, her eyes wide like huge, sparkling emeralds as she listened to Drew outlining plans for another fashion show in New York next year.

'You certainly seem to be a success even before you have exhibited,' said Claude, leaning forward enthusiastically. 'Seats for your show are like gold dust. We nearly had a riot on our hands today when we said they were all taken.'

Amanda grinned. 'I think maybe that's thanks to good publicity rather than my talent.'

'That reminds me, Drew,' Marion suddenly interrupted, putting down her glass of cognac, 'there was a phone call for you when I was in the office. A Mademoiselle Jordan Lee.' She frowned. 'Have I got the name right?'

'Yes, Jordan,' Drew said easily. 'Did she leave a message?'

Amanda could feel her whole body stiffen at the mention of the other woman.

'She wished to know if it would be possible for her to attend the fashion show.' Marion's mouth turned down expressively. 'I told her all the seats were now taken, but she insisted that you should ring her to discuss it.'

'I'll ring her later. I'm sure we can arrange something as she's so anxious,' Drew said smoothly.

After that the talk and laughter went over Amanda's head. She felt a knife twist inside her so savagely, it was an effort not to cry out in pain. So Drew was going to ensure that his wife-to-be had a seat to select the wedding dress of her choice.

Suddenly she became aware that Marion was talking to her across the table and she hadn't heard a word she had said.

'Are you all right, Amanda?' the French girl asked in concern.

'Yes, of course,' said Amanda quickly, conscious of Drew's dark eyes resting on her. 'I—I'm sorry, Marion, but I think I'm just tired.'

The girl nodded, accepting the explanation easily. 'Yes, we have been working long hours lately, I think we will all collapse with fatigue after the show.'

'If you will all excuse me, I think I'll retire for the evening.' Amanda smiled wanly, trying not to notice the worried frown on Drew's face.

She jumped nervously as he placed a solicitous hand on her arm. 'I'll escort you.'

'No!' Her voice was sharper than she realised, and she was mindful of the curious faces watching them as she put some warmth back into her voice. 'No, Drew, honestly, I wouldn't be happy if I cut your evening short.' Quickly she turned away to say goodnight to the others so that he didn't have a chance to argue.

Her every nerve was tense as she walked away from them across the room. She could feel Drew's eyes watching her, could almost feel them physically touching the bare skin of her back. She swallowed hard and forced herself to walk slowly until the large gilded doors closed behind her, then she lifted up her skirts and fled down the empty corridor towards the private lift.

Amanda had her key out ready to open the door to the apartment as the lift stopped on the top floor. But she was surprised to find that she didn't need it, as the door was slightly ajar. She paused for a moment, frowning; she had been last to leave the apartment and she was sure she had closed the door firmly behind her. Shrugging, she put her key back in her bag and went in. Probably a member of staff had been in and forgotten to close it.

The apartment was completely dark except for the flickering orange light that the fire was casting over the walls of the lounge. She flicked a light switch on the wall, but it was the wrong one for the room and lit the outside patio instead. Sighing, she moved across towards the lamp on the coffee-table. She was mid-way across the room when a sudden sound coming from the direction of the bedrooms made her freeze. There was someone else in the apartment!

She felt a prickle of fear creep down her spine as she stood in the darkened room and listened. It couldn't be a member of staff, they would have switched all the lights on and called to her as she came in. There was deathly silence except for the loud thud of her heartbeat, and the shadows from the fire played eerily over the room like unearthly dancing figures. Even though she couldn't hear anything else, she knew she wasn't alone, she could feel the small hairs on the back of her neck tingle with that awareness. For one moment she didn't know whether she should move forward and switch on the light or move back towards the door.

Fear made her choose the door and she whirled around, her heart pounding unmercifully hard. That fear turned to blind terror as she collided with the solid figure of a man emerging from the bedrooms.

For a moment she was transfixed with shock. It held her paralysed, so that all she could do was stare with wide eyes at the dark, shadowy figure, dressed all in black. She couldn't see his face, he was wearing a bala-clava; only the threatening glitter of razor-sharp eyes showed. Then he backed away into the shadows and out of the door.

Amanda fell back against the wall, shaking. She couldn't move, she couldn't think straight, she was so frightened. She didn't know how long she stood like that; it could only have been minutes, but it felt like an eternity. Then the door opened and bright golden light flooded over her and she saw Drew's familiar, reassuring figure.

'Amanda! What's the matter? What's happened?' His tone was immediately concerned, his eyes taking in her distress at a glance.

'Some—someone has broken in.' Her voice quivered precariously. 'He was here when I came in.'

'Are you all right?' he asked sharply, coming over, his face grim, his eyes raking over her in quick assessment.

'Yes.' Her voice broke on a sob as he cradled her in the warm circle of his arms.

'It's all right, darling, it's all right.' His voice was low and calm and it helped to stem the tremors that racked her body. He swept her up into his arms then, and carried her easily into her bedroom. She could feel the strength of his muscles as she leaned her head against him.

'Our intruder doesn't seem to have disturbed much,' Drew observed as he placed her gently down on her bed. For a moment she was unwilling to relinquish her hold on him and her arms clung around his neck, needing him.

'It's all right, sweetheart, I'm not going anywhere.' Gently he moved her arms from him and then stood up to pick up the phone beside the bed. 'I'm just going to ring Security. What was the man wearing, Amanda? Can you remember what he looked like?'

She shook her head helplessly. 'It was dark, he—he wore a balaclava.'

'Which door did he leave by?' Drew asked quickly.

'The main one.'

Drew nodded. 'He must have used the fire escape. He's probably well gone by now, but I'll get Security to check.'

Amanda watched him as he talked on the phone. She couldn't understand a word of his rapid French, but somehow the calm, decisive way he spoke instilled new strength into her. Her eyes wandered around the room. Very little had been disturbed. The wardrobe doors were open and some of her clothes were on the floor, but it didn't look as if anything had been taken. Her jewellery was still sitting on the dressing-table.

Drew replaced the phone and stared down at her grimly. 'Whoever it was had an accomplice. The office has also been broken into.'

Amanda sat bolt upright. 'My designs—have they...'

Drew shook his head, quickly soothing her. 'The only reason they managed to get in at all is because I have a lot of my security force guarding your designs.'

Amanda leaned back against her pillows. 'Do you think that was what they were after?'

'Oh, without doubt. Your collection has received a lot of publicity and interest. I should think whoever broke in here tonight was hoping to find your designs and make a quick fortune spinning off copies.' The phone rang and he snatched it up impatiently, a frown etching the stern lines of his face. He spoke calmly, but Amanda could feel his anger and she could sense that some members of his staff would feel the sharp edge of his tongue about the breach of security. Drew was a man who prided himself in a top-class workforce; he wouldn't tolerate negligence or sloppy work easily—if at all.

'Well, it's as I thought. They seem to have made their escape through the fire exits,' Drew said, replacing the receiver.

'You don't—don't think they'll come back, do you?' She clenched her hands nervously. His eyes softened as he looked down at the porcelain whiteness of her skin.

'I don't think they would be that stupid. Surveillance will be razor-sharp around here after this.' He sat back down on the bed beside her. 'How do you feel now?'

'Fine,' she answered huskily.

'Sure?' His eyes narrowed on her searchingly. 'You looked so——' he paused for a moment as if searching for the right word '—anguished, when you left the table this evening.'

'Is that why you followed me up?' she asked him breathlessly.

'Partly.' He stroked a wave of gold hair back from her face. 'I've been working you too hard lately,' he murmured. There was a deep tenderness in his voice and Amanda had to swallow hard to keep a tight rein on the answering emotions which welled up inside her.

'I'll be fine.' Her eyes were over-bright as she looked up at him. 'There's nothing wrong with me that a good night's sleep won't cure.' And that must be the biggest understatement of the year, she thought wretchedly; if I sleep from now until doomsday I'll never get over him.

Drew nodded and stood up, but he still hesitated, looking down at her. 'Why don't you put a call through to Bermuda and speak to James? It might make you feel better,' he suggested, a sombre look belying the kindness of his words.

'I—I don't think so.' For a moment her eyes were wide, unguarded as she looked up at him. The only thing that would make her feel better was to have his solid warmth next to her, holding her for ever. But that was wishing for the impossible. 'Maybe tomorrow.' Her eyelashes fluttered down.

'Goodnight, Amanda.' His voice was polite and distant. 'I'll get someone to come up and straighten things up for you in here.'

Before she could tell him that there was no need, that she was perfectly able to see to things herself, he was gone.

In fact Amanda was glad of the girl he sent in. She could speak no English and just got on with her work quietly and efficiently, straightening the room, picking all the clothes off the floor, even running Amanda a bath.

Amanda felt thoroughly spoilt as she stepped back into the bedroom and found the room perfect, the bed-clothes turned down, even a bedtime drink waiting for her.

She lay awake for ages in the huge bed, tossing and turning. She was exhausted, but her troubled mind wouldn't let her relax, and finally she drifted into a deep, uneasy sleep.

In her dreams she was walking through the apartment. She knew Drew was there somewhere and she was desperately searching for him. Everything was dark, silent and strangely terrifying. Then suddenly she could see the man again in his dark mask, cold, grey eyes lunging down at her, and she knew Drew wasn't going to save her, Drew was with Jordan.

She awoke in darkness and in blind panic, tears streaming down her face, Drew's name on her lips. Someone was in her room, and as the dark shadow came nearer she struggled wildly to escape from the covers of her bed. The shadow was right next to her and she struck out in a useless attempt to fight him off.

A light flicked on, dispelling the frightening visions, and it was Drew's handsome face that was looking down at her.

CHAPTER ELEVEN

'OH, DREW, I thought—I——' Amanda's breath was catching raggedly, so that she could hardly speak.

He slipped his arms around her with infinite care and held her close, stroking her hair soothingly as if she were a child. 'It's all right, Amanda, it was only a bad dream.'

'Yes, but I was so frightened.' She trembled against him. 'I thought that man had come back, I could see him!' she shuddered.

'There's no one here and I won't let anyone harm you.' His voice was gentle and reassuring.

She relaxed against him. She could hear the steady beat of his heart, smell the lovely faint traces of his cologne, and she snuggled closer. He held her like that for a moment, then his muscles seemed to tauten and he guided her gently back against the pillows and looked searchingly down at her. 'Feel better now?'

She nodded, for the first time realising that he was wearing only a short white towelling robe, which hung open at his chest. His skin gleamed a majestic study of bronze in the lamplight. 'I'm sorry I woke you.'

He grinned down at her. 'You were certainly screaming my name loud enough. I thought someone was in here attacking you.'

She flushed a deep crimson. 'I'm sorry,' she whispered.

'Don't worry about it, I was awake anyway.' He reached out a hand to switch the lamp off. 'Now try and get some sleep.'

Panic swept through her as he stood up to leave her. She didn't want to be left alone in the dark. She wanted to ask him to stay with her. 'Drew?' she began nervously.

He paused by the door. 'Yes?'

'Will—will you leave the light on outside?' She couldn't find the courage to ask what she really wanted.

'Yes.'

He turned to go and she found herself blurting out, 'Don't go, Drew,' in a panic-stricken voice.

He turned slowly to look at her but said nothing.

'Please don't go,' she asked in a trembling voice. 'I'm just so frightened. I want you to stay with me.'

'You don't know what you're asking,' he told her harshly.

'I—I need you, Drew. I don't want to be on my own tonight.' She felt like a little girl wanting security and warmth, which was absurd. Wanting those things from Drew was about as safe as inviting a panther into your bed. 'I just want you to hold me,' she begged softly, not caring what she was inviting as long as she had his reassuring presence to shut the nightmares out.

He swore softly under his breath. 'I'm not made of stone, Amanda.'

'No, I'm sorry.' She sank down against her pillows, suddenly feeling incredibly foolish. 'Forget I asked.'

'How can I forget that?' He moved back into the room and sat beside her on the edge of the bed. 'You've just admitted to needing me; that's not something I can dismiss lightly to the back of my mind.'

'Well, just pretend I didn't mean it,' she whispered desolately.

He caught hold of her shoulder and suddenly his voice was rough and angry. 'But you did mean it.' He shook her slightly. 'Didn't you, Amanda?'

She drew in a long, shuddering breath and nodded.

'Say it, Amanda.' His grip was tight and painful.

'Yes, Drew—yes, I need you.' Her voice trembled with emotion.

There was silence for a moment and he let his hold on her relax. 'Was that really so difficult for you to admit?'

She brushed a hand roughly over her face as tears threatened. 'You—you know it was.'

He stared at her for a moment. 'That is one hell of a barrier you've built up around you,' he said wonderingly. 'Do you try to keep your emotions locked away from everybody, or is just me?'

She didn't answer him, she couldn't, because suddenly it occurred to her that he was right, she did try to close herself away from people. She had done ever since her engagement to Drew had ended. She had been so determined that no one was going to get the chance to hurt her again that she had isolated herself away, hiding behind her work. Her thoughts froze for a moment. Wasn't that what she had always done, as far back as the time when her mother had left home? Even then she had withdrawn into herself, unable to face rejection.

Drew pulled back the covers slightly. 'Let's try and get some sleep, shall we?' He sounded weary all of a sudden. She felt the bed sink slightly as he climbed in beside her.

For a long time she lay in the darkness, stiffly apart from him. His breathing was deep and regular and she listened to it for a while, wondering if he was wide awake, as she was.

'When do you intend marrying James?' he asked suddenly.

Amanda looked over towards him startled, unsure of how to answer. 'I—I haven't set a date for anything,' she said at last.

'Think before you do,' he told her drily. 'Because I don't think he's right for you—I don't think you love him.'

Her heart hammered painfully, her mouth felt dry. 'What makes you such an expert on what's right for me?'

He rolled over on his side to stare at her through the darkness. 'Observation,' he stated obliquely. 'I've watched you both together; there doesn't seem to be any warmth or tenderness when you look at him. You know, Amanda, I think you're afraid of love.'

'My goodness, you are observant,' she was stung to reply contemptuously.

'You're afraid, so you've agreed to marry a man for whom you have no deep feelings because you think it's a safe way out,' he continued as if she hadn't spoken. 'You think because you don't love him he won't be able to hurt you. But that's the quickest road to disaster, Amanda. You shouldn't contemplate marriage to someone unless you love them with all your heart.'

Tears sprang to her eyes. The way he did Jordan? She couldn't bear to listen to any more.

'Just shut up, Drew, you don't know what you're talking about.'

'I know that James doesn't deserve you. He hasn't made one attempt to contact you while you've been here,' he went on harshly, ignoring the pain in her voice.

'I don't damn well care!' She flew at him, her hands beating against his chest, tears falling in an unremitting stream down her face. She was tired, so tired of pretending. The weariness of the last few weeks, combined with the traumatic events of the evening, had drained her of everything. Now all she wanted was to be in Drew's arms. Suddenly she wanted to forget that he didn't love her, wanted to throw her pride away and just cling to him. 'I don't care, do you hear me?' Her tears fell on the taut muscles of his chest as he caught hold of her hands.

'Amanda, for God's sake stop it, don't cry like that. I didn't mean to hurt you,' he said gently, trying to stem the tide of her anguish. But she had lost all control, all the barriers that she had so carefully built around her collapsing into splintered pieces. Moving into the wide protective circle of his arms, she buried her head against the smoothness of his chest and wept copious tears. 'I shall never marry James—never.' Her words were muffled, incoherent. 'I've never loved him, you were right when you said that—that——'

'What?' Drew stroked the tears away from her lips. 'Sweetheart, what are you saying? I can't make out one word.'

She looked up at the blurred shadows of his face. 'I said you were right—I don't love James.' Her voice was still catching with sobs, and for a moment when he didn't make any reply she thought he still hadn't heard her. 'And I'm afraid,' she tagged on lamely.

Anything else she had been going to say was crushed as he brought her close against his body. 'Don't be, Amanda; now that you've faced up to that, everything will be all right.' His voice sounded deep and husky with emotion.

'No, it won't, nothing will ever be right again,' she whispered brokenly. She drank in the clean male aroma of him, savouring every moment in his arms, the delicious feeling of her skin against his. How could things ever be all right when he was going to marry someone else, when she would never spend all her nights like this?

Through the undrawn curtains a shaft of moonlight fell across the bed, illuminating the white silk sheets, the tousled gold of her hair. She looked up at his strong features and felt her throat tighten, feeling dizzy as she held his gaze. She could see the dark desire in his eyes and she was filled with an unbearable longing for him to touch her, to caress her. Her body burnt as if she were suffering from a fever only he could satisfy.

She reached up a trembling hand and traced the firm line of his jaw wonderingly. He hesitated only momentarily before his mouth came down on her hairline, brushing it with gentle kisses. She brought both her arms up and around his neck, and her fingers burrowed into his dark, thick hair as she pressed her body even closer against his.

'Love me,' she whispered as she moved her head, searching for his lips, needing to feel them against hers.

All her pride and caution was abandoned, her barriers torn away. Even though Drew didn't love her, even though she probably would be devastated tomorrow when he would calmly and remotely walk away from her—she needed him tonight.

He rolled across her and his lips met hers with a fierce, passionate intensity that left her weak with desire and love. His hands moved down over the soft white night-dress, unfastening it easily, leaving her naked and vulnerable to him.

Amanda wondered if she was dreaming as she looked up at the forceful contours of Drew's face, granite-hard in the half-light. For a moment he just looked at her, his eyes taking in every curve of her body. 'You're so beautiful,' he breathed huskily.

Her response to him was without inhibition. She lifted her arms up towards him. 'I want you, Drew,' she said softly, her body aching to have him back against her.

'We need to talk before——' The rest of his words were cut off as she reached up to him, pressing her naked body against his. She didn't want him to say anything, she couldn't bear it if he was about to make it clear he didn't love her, that he was going to marry someone else. She didn't want any rational thoughts to spoil this moment. 'I don't want to talk, Drew.' She nibbled his ear tormentingly. 'I want to make love.'

'God, Amanda!' he groaned hoarsely, then he was raining urgent kisses over her face and throat and breasts. 'You don't know how it makes me feel to hear you say that to me after all this time.'

She moaned a little in sheer ecstasy at the familiar feel of him against her. How many nights had she lain awake raw with longing for him? She loved him from the very depths of her soul. Wanted him to make her feel part of him, wanted him to hold her close for ever.

'I need you, Drew,' she breathed against his skin, pressing her lips into the hollow of his throat. Those were the last coherent words she was able to utter for quite some time, as Drew took total possession of her body.

His lovemaking seemed to open the floodgates to a storm of passion. It was as if they just couldn't get enough of each other. They were lost in a whirlpool of desire at first urgent and powerful, then tender and so overwhelmingly gentle that she found that she was sobbing—her emotions overflowing with a mixture of joy and bittersweet anguish.

As if he understood, Drew held her close afterwards, cradling her until her breathing was steady and she drifted into a deep and wonderful sleep.

When she awoke she was lying entwined in Drew's arms, with only the silk sheets covering their naked bodies. The grey light of dawn had turned a pearly pink, giving everything an ethereal, unreal quality. Outside she could hear the faint hum of Paris; some bells were ringing somewhere and her lips curved in a smile—they seemed to echo the joy that was ringing out inside her body. If she had a wish now, she would wish that time could stop here. That she could lie for ever in Drew's arms and close the rest of the world out. She stirred a little, stretching her head up to kiss the pulse beating in the strong column of his throat.

'Mmm. Do that again and you might get more than you bargained for.' Drew's voice was deep and warm, and it sent a new wave of desire flooding through her body.

She looked up at him, her eyes wide and sea-green. 'Maybe that's what I want,' she told him throatily.

He smiled that slow, lazy smile that turned her heart over. Then he moved to claim the soft, inviting curve of her mouth. The covers fell to one side as his hand slid from her waist to her breast, cupping it through the silky material of the sheets. He moved her slightly, so that she was lying over him, the smooth skin of her back against his powerful chest. 'I thought you were never going to wake up,' he whispered huskily against the sensitive skin of her neck, and then kissed her there, making her writhe in delight. She stretched her arms back to link them around his neck in a spontaneous gesture that raised her breasts. She heard Drew's sudden intake of breath, then his caresses became more demanding, his kisses more intense. She groaned and rolled over, desire engulfing her in a deep ache of need, and she wondered at the incredible way he was able to arouse her after a night of passion that had so completely fulfilled her.

'I—I can hear music,' she murmured dreamily against his lips. Then to her surprise she heard him groan with irritation.

'It's the telephone.'

'Let's just ignore it.' She snuggled close against him, suddenly afraid of any outside intrusion. He grinned and kissed her. But the phone kept on ringing shrilly; whoever was at the other end wasn't going to give up.

Swearing under his breath, Drew finally reached out an impatient hand and snatched it up. 'Yes?' he snapped out angrily.

Amanda, lying with her head against his chest, could feel his muscles tighten abruptly. 'Jordan!' He sounded surprised, and the next minute he was moving away from her to sit on the edge of the bed. 'What about the designs waiting to be shipped?' he asked abruptly.

Staring at the forceful contours of his broad, smooth back, Amanda wondered how she could suddenly feel so icy cold after such a raging heat had been burning her body.

'All right, Jordan, don't panic, I'll get the first available flight back to London.'

Amanda could hardly bring herself to look at him as he put the receiver down, afraid that he would see the unhappy shadows that filled her green eyes.

'Someone broke into the Hunter building last night. The manager was working late and discovered them trying to break into the strong-room,' he told her grimly.

'Is he all right?' Her eyes flew anxiously to his now.

Drew nodded. 'Suffering from shock, but apart from that—they tied him up while they finished searching the place.' He raked an angry hand through thick, dark hair. 'It looks as if they were in league with the ones who broke in here last night.'

'And the designs?' She sat up a little, clutching the white sheet tightly over her breasts.

He gave her a bleak smile. 'Luckily I rang George last night and suggested they be moved. That was why he'd been working late.' He reached out a hand and picked up the phone again. 'I'm going to have to go back to London. They're panicking now about the shipment of the designs.' He spoke in French as someone answered, and for the next few moments Amanda was completely in the dark as to what was going on.

'They have some seats available,' he told her when he finally put the phone down. Hope flared in her—did he want to take her with him? 'Will you be able to cope with things here?' he went on to ask, and all hopes were dashed. She nodded, but this time she couldn't hide the anguish in her eyes.

There was silence as he looked at her for a moment. Her skin was flushed from the warmth of his love-making, her hair tumbled over her bare shoulders in golden fiery profusion. 'God, I don't want to leave you, Amanda,' he breathed, leaning over to kiss her waiting lips. At once desire ignited inside her and she was clinging to him, her lips ardent and aroused.

When he moved away from her his breathing was slightly ragged and there was regret in his dark eyes. 'There's so much that we have to sort out between us. So much that we haven't said. I'm going to try and get back tonight.' He tipped her chin gently. 'Book a table in the restaurant for us around nine-thirty—or, better still, order room service.' He finished huskily, 'I want to continue where we left off.'

She gave him a tremulous smile and he moved away. 'Now, I've got to hurry. This flight I'm booked on leaves in three-quarters of an hour.' He picked up his robe from the floor and moved across the room. She couldn't help admiring the superb, muscular lines of his body as he moved with the grace and power of an athlete. He turned and caught her eye and grinned. 'Get some sleep, Amanda, you're going to need all your energy for tonight.'

She flushed a deep, warm red as she lay back against the pillows, but she couldn't relax. She could hear Drew as he turned the shower on in his bathroom and then as he moved around his room. She knew he had to go back to London, but it still hurt, because deep down she knew that, as well as work, he was going back to Jordan.

She sighed and threw back the sheets; she couldn't lie there tormenting herself with those thoughts. He had said he would come back tonight; that must mean something, surely?

She selected a silk jade-coloured kimono and belted it tightly around her narrow waist before stepping out into the apartment. Drew was still in his room, so she made her way into the kitchen to make them both a cup of coffee. She was just bringing it down to him when he stepped into the lounge. He was dressed in a dark business suit and crisp white shirt with a grey silk tie. She lowered her gaze, finding this devastating change from lover to top businessman unsettling. 'I—I've made you a drink,' she told him shyly.

'You should be in bed,' he admonished, putting his briefcase down, but he looked pleased as he took the china cup and saucer from her. 'Thanks, honey.' He didn't bother to sit down, but quickly swallowed the contents of the delicate cup.

'Aren't you going to have something to eat before you go?' As she looked up at him it occurred to her that she sounded like a wife, and she flushed.

'No time.' He put his cup down and pulled her closer. 'Don't worry, I'll be well looked after.'

She wanted to deny that she was worried, but a lump rose in her throat. She was worried, she hated him going anywhere without her—which was absolutely absurd. Then his lips were covering hers, and she gave a small moan as she pressed close against him, winding her hands up around his shoulders to curl them through his thick, dark hair.

'Temptress,' he whispered, his voice thick with desire as he pulled away from her. 'I'll see you tonight.' The way he said those words made her shiver with little thrills of excitement. She wondered if this was what it would be like to be married to Drew. Nights filled with passion, mornings when she would watch him leave with the thrilling anticipation of his return. Then her heart lurched and she felt that inexplicable coldness. It wouldn't be she who would share Drew's life like that, it would be Jordan. Jealousy twisted like a cold blade inside her.

Drew picked up his briefcase and walked with her towards the glass sliding doors to the roof garden. 'Don't come out, Amanda, you'll catch cold.'

As she looked questioningly up at him, he smiled. 'I'm taking the helicopter. It's quicker than driving to the airport.' And as her eyes widened apprehensively he squeezed her arm. 'Don't worry, I'll be back before you know it.' Then he was stepping out of the doors and, with a last wave towards her, hurrying to climb inside the huge, gleaming monster.

She stepped outside to watch him, ignoring his words. It was a cold, sharp day, and all traces of the warm spring weather that the city had been enjoying over the last few weeks had gone. It was like winter all over again. Drew started up the engines of the helicopter and the powerful blades whirled through the air, whipping up a breeze that ruffled the blue water of the swimming pool and made Amanda's russet hair fly about her face in disarray.

She pushed it back impatiently and held the delicate silk of her kimono tightly around her shivering body as the aircraft rose smoothly away from the roof and swung over the edge. She watched as it wavered slightly as Drew turned it. Then it was whirling away out over the Paris skyline. She moved further out to the stone balustrade and watched until it was a mere speck and then disappeared. Her heart was hammering painfully; it had terrified her watching him manoeuvre that machine, even though he had done it expertly, and had probably done it thousands of times before. God, she hoped he would be safe! She turned to go back into the warmth of the building. Just say something happened to him? Her fingers curled into tight balls. She couldn't bear it—she couldn't live without him. Her mind froze. She was going to have to live without him, Drew didn't belong to her.

CHAPTER TWELVE

AMANDA tried to concentrate on her work that day. There were so many things to do. The model agency had sent over a lot of girls for her to look over. They were all sitting outside the office waiting for her at ten o'clock, and she had a pile of work on her desk.

Before she did anything, though, she rang the restaurant manager and asked him to reserve a table for her and Drew this evening. Drew was right, they did need to talk. He had said this morning that he wanted them to continue like that. Had he meant as lovers, after he married Jordan? she wondered. He was very French in a lot of his ways, and the French thought nothing of having a lover when they were married. To them it was the sophisticated thing to do. She searched her desk angrily for the portfolio of the first girl she was to see. Could she really live her life in the shadow of Drew's wife? As much as she loved him, she knew she could not.

The models Amanda interviewed were mostly English and American; they were taller than the French girls, better for fashion work. Most of them were already highly skilled in the art of runway, where a model had to change at the speed of light in a space the size of a telephone kiosk and then move with the unruffled elegance of a gazelle down the catwalk.

After talking briefly with each of them, Amanda brought them into the large conference pavilion where the long catwalk had been set up for the fashion show. The electricians were still working on the lighting systems and she got one of them to set the lights on the catwalk and switch on snatches of the music they had selected for the show while each of the girls walked down it.

Marion came and stood next to Amanda, watching the girls with interest.

'They are good!' she exclaimed, tapping her foot to a gyrating rock variation of 'Here Comes the Bride'.

'Yes,' Amanda agreed, but her voice sounded dull and flat. She couldn't seem to raise any enthusiasm for anything.

'You don't agree?' The French girl was quick to pick up the tone in Amanda's voice and she turned surprised eyes on her.

'They're wonderful,' Amanda reiterated, and signalled to the lighting technician to cut the music. Immediately everything died, the lights and the music. Amanda's lips twisted wryly; that was a lot like how she felt inside.

Leaving Marion, she walked over to have another few words with the girls before they left.

Marion was waiting for her as she turned to go back to the office. 'Is everything all right, Amanda?' she asked, falling into step beside her.

'Yes, of course.' Amanda tried to keep her voice light. She glanced at her gold wristwatch and wondered where Drew would be now.

'Drew should be in London now,' said Marion as though reading her mind. Amanda shot her a startled glance and she laughed. 'Yes, it is that obvious,' she said to the unspoken question on Amanda's face. 'To a French girl, anyway. Don't forget that we French are perceptive when it comes to *affaires d'amour*. I have suspected for some time, but I was certain when I watched you together at the dining-table last night. There was such love in your eyes.'

Amanda winced with embarrassment. Had everyone noticed? she wondered.

'Then, when Drew rang me this morning...' The French girl gave an expressive shrug.

'Drew rang you?' Amanda stopped walking and turned to look at the other girl.

'Yes, from the airport. He asked me to keep an eye on you and make sure you didn't do too much work. He was so concerned about you. Last night, too, when you left the dining-table looking so pale.'

'Was he?' It was amazing how that little piece of information made her feel so warm inside. Pathetic how she could grasp at the slightest indication that Drew's feelings for her might be genuine; but she did. That conversation with Marion kept her going through the day with a glow of happiness in her heart.

She kept glancing at the clock in the office, counting the hours until his return. At six she finished work and went up to the apartment to shower and get ready.

She chose a dress from her own collection of 'After Dark' evening dresses. It was black taffeta, plain yet so cleverly cut that it enhanced every sensual line of her body and heightened her golden, fiery beauty. Her only jewellery was a string of entwined, beautifully matched pearls that Drew had brought back for her from a trip to one of his hotels in the South Sea Islands. As she fastened the diamond clasp on them she remembered Drew fastening them around her neck all that time ago.

'How about the South Seas for our honeymoon?' he had whispered, kissing the tender skin above the pearls and working his way up towards her lips. Amanda shivered a little now as she remembered those passionate kisses. She hadn't been able to wear this necklace after their engagement had ended, although her hand had always lingered over it before choosing something else.

She turned away from her reflection and went into the lounge. The lights were dimmed, the fire blazed invitingly. Outside, the roof garden was fully lit ready for Drew's return. Amanda poured herself a glass of wine and sat in the soft, deep settee to wait.

Half-past nine came and went, and as the clock ticked inexorably past ten and towards eleven Amanda's thoughts turned from tender reflections to memories of other times when she had sat waiting for Drew, wondering where he was, who he was with.

The phone rang shrilly and she jumped to answer it, hoping it was Drew—hoping he would tell her he loved her and he was on his way. It was the restaurant manager, enquiring whether or not he should hold their table for them any longer. She thanked him, told him Drew had been detained and to just let the table go.

When she put the phone down there were tears in her eyes. This was all so familiar. Drew was probably still in London with Jordan, and here she was hurting inside, making excuses for his absence.

She picked up her wineglass from the table and brought it into the kitchen. There was no point sitting waiting any longer. She might as well go to bed. Maybe tomorrow her thoughts would be rational enough for her to decide what to do.

She was just moving to switch off the lounge lights when she heard the distant whirl of the helicopter. Her heart leapt painfully and she crossed to the windows to look out. Sure enough, the aircraft was making its descent on to the roof, its lights blazing powerfully through the velvet black of the sky. Amanda swallowed hard and closed her eyes. He had come back.

The engine noise grew louder and then faded to a soft whine as the machine settled safely down. Amanda moved back into the shadows of the room, her heart thumping wildly. She didn't know if she wanted to fling herself into his arms or if she should coolly tell him she was tired and on her way to bed. Her lips curved in a mocking smile; who was she kidding? She knew exactly what she wanted to do, and coldness didn't come into it. The doors opened behind her and she turned, a smile of anticipation lighting her features. But that smile died rapidly as she came face to face with Jordan!

'Well, hello, Amanda,' the woman drawled mockingly. 'You waited up for us—how sweet!'

Amanda's eyes moved to the doors behind her, searching for Drew. 'Drew's just getting my luggage,' said Jordan, moving further into the room. She looked strikingly beautiful in a black leather suit. The skirt clung to her narrow hips, the jacket open slightly, showing an alluring glimpse of voluptuous breasts under a white silk blouse. Her honey-blonde hair was swept dramatically over one shoulder and fell in flowing curls to her waist.

'Amanda, you're still up!' Drew's surprised voice distracted her attention away from the other woman. He looked so fantastic, framed in the doorway against the Paris skyline. Was it only this morning that she had clung to him, kissing him with all the love and passion that he so easily aroused in her with just one glance? 'I'm sorry I'm later than I said, but we were delayed at the airport.' He put down Jordan's suitcase and crossed the room towards her.

He was delayed with Jordan. Her brain had to relay the message clearly to her heart so that she turned her face as he reached her side, receiving his kiss on her cheek. She could see the dark, questioning light in his eyes as he straightened and her eyes glittered furiously. What did he expect, that she should allow him to kiss her coolly on the lips in front of his fiancée? God, the man had a real nerve!

'We managed to sort everything out about the travelling arrangements for the collection,' he told her calmly, moving across to the drinks cabinet.

'Good,' she said flatly.

'Would you like a drink, Amanda?' he asked smoothly as if she hadn't spoken. She shook her head and watched with a rising anger as Jordan said she would have her usual and Drew poured her a glass of whisky without any hesitation. That casual knowledge of her taste in drinks seemed to speak volumes about their relationship.

'If you'll both excuse me, I'll go to bed.' She backed away a little. 'I was just on my way when you arrived back.'

'Don't go, Amanda.' Drew's eyes were gentle as he looked across at her; she noticed the tired lines etched a little on his strong face and her heart constricted. 'We've got a lot of things to discuss,' he said meaningfully.

She hesitated and then nodded.

'Good.' He smiled and then turned to Jordan. 'I'll just ring down and arrange a room for you. Are you hungry? Should I order room service for you?' The concerned note in his voice twisted the blade of jealousy deep inside Amanda.

'Why don't you both go down to the restaurant? I'm sure the manager will find you a cosy table for two,' she suggested in a brittle tone.

Drew shot her a narrow-eyed look. 'It's good of you to be concerned, Amanda, but I'm not hungry.' He crossed the room and picked up the telephone.

Jordan lounged back in her chair as he spoke in rapid French, arranging things for her. 'Drew is wonderful, organising everything so I could come over for the fashion show.' Her blue eyes glittered and a gloating little smile played around her lips as she looked over at Amanda. 'I can hardly wait to choose my dress, and of course to wear it.'

'I'm sure you can't,' Amanda said coldly.

Drew put down the phone and turned. 'Well, there's a room on the ground floor,' he said. 'I'll just get your other case from the helicopter, then we'll go down.'

There was silence for a moment when he had left the room. Then Jordan turned cold blue eyes up towards Amanda. 'Have you enjoyed your stay in Paris?'

'It's been hard work, but yes, I have enjoyed it.' Amanda's voice was icy and very wary.

'Oh, I'm sure Drew hasn't overworked you, you're such an asset to the company.'

'And just what do you mean by that?' Amanda was fast losing her cool at the woman's condescending manner.

Jordan's delicately arched eyebrows rose. 'Why, I was being complimentary, Amanda. I've just finished my financial report on Hunter Fashions, and one thing I noticed was just how valuable you are to the business; it wouldn't be the same without you. I'm sure Drew is well aware of the fact and has treated you accordingly.'

'How lovely that you should be so very concerned about me,' said Amanda coldly, matching Jordan's equivocal air.

Jordan frowned and the polite mask slipped, showing a glimpse of the venom beneath. 'I'm not concerned about you at all. I just thought I would make things very clear so that you didn't get the wrong idea about Drew.'

'Oh, I think I get the idea,' Amanda replied calmly.

'Idea about what?' Drew made them both jump as he came back into the room. He put down Jordan's case and rubbed his hands. 'God, it's cold out there! I had to cover the swimming pool over, I think it might actually freeze tonight.' He grinned at Amanda. 'Now, what are these ideas you've had?'

Jordan practically shot off her chair. 'Drew, I'm so tired, do you think we could go down now?'

'Yes, of course.' Drew moved his glance sharply to the other woman. Then he picked up one of her bags. 'We'll get room service to bring the rest of them down,' he told her easily as they crossed towards the door. 'I'll see you later, Amanda,' he muttered before they both disappeared.

'I bet.' Amanda's voice was barely a whisper, her green eyes wide with hurt. She wouldn't be surprised if Drew didn't come back to the apartment tonight. After all, she knew they slept together; Jordan probably was used to staying with Drew in his bedroom in the apartment. Her presence must be really cramping their style.

For a while she stood, desolate, not knowing what to do with herself. If she started to cry she didn't think she would ever stop. She loved Drew so much, but he would never return those feelings. If Jordan was to be believed, he didn't care about her at all, he was just stringing her along so that she wouldn't leave the business at such a critical time. Then she remembered the tender way he had kissed her last night and her heart constricted. Surely no man could make love like that if there were no feelings involved?

She buried her head in her hands; she had to think rationally. Look at the facts coldly: Drew was downstairs with Jordan right now, probably making love to her at this very moment, and he had made it very clear the day he took over Hunter Fashions that his interest in her was as a designer, nothing else.

Those thoughts drove Amanda towards her bedroom. She knew now that she couldn't stay here any longer, couldn't bear to be in the same building as Drew knowing he was with another woman; the woman he was going to marry. She opened her wardrobe and started to pull her clothes out. She would take a taxi to the airport and take the first available flight back to London. Her brain moved ahead, planning what she would do when she got there: get another job, find some way to break the news to her father gently. She had to keep her mind busy—keep out the pain and hopelessness that was waiting to seep in.

She couldn't find her passport; she turned out all the drawers in the dressing-table and writing bureau, but it wasn't there. She ran a flustered hand through her long hair—where on earth had she left it? Trying to remain calm, she retraced her steps into the lounge. Perhaps Drew had taken it from her and put it in his desk. She opened up the polished rosewood cover and was in the process of going through Drew's papers when the door opened beside her.

'Lost something?' Drew's light, bantering tone belied the scrutinising darkness of his eyes. She swung her head around in shock and surprise, for a moment she couldn't find her voice to answer him. Absurdly, she felt guilty about her invasion into his private things.

'No—well, yes.' She turned towards him, lifting her chin defiantly. She had nothing to feel guilty about—unlike him. 'Actually, I was looking for my passport.'

'I see.' His tone had hardened and he walked towards her with a purposeful stride that made her back away. He stopped at the desk and closed the lid with a resounding slam. 'Are you going to tell me why you're looking for your passport tonight of all nights?'

'I wasn't aware that tonight was anything special.' She folded her arms to stop them trembling and looked at him with wide-eyed indifference.

She could see the storm-clouds gathering in his face, his brow furrowing deeply, his mouth a cruel straight line. 'All right, Amanda, let's have it,' he grated harshly. 'What's the matter with you?'

'The matter?' she echoed, and her voice rose as she fought with herself for control. 'What makes you think there's something wrong? I'm just tired. I think I'll go to bed now.' She turned to leave him, blindly wanting to escape.

'Stop right there.' His deep, commanding voice made her freeze. 'We did away with all those barriers last night. You can't put them back up again, Amanda; you can't walk away and pretend nothing happened.'

'But it's all right for you to pretend, isn't it, Drew?' she said obliquely. 'You seem to be able to throw yourself into your business life and your personal life with equal feeling.'

'Amanda, you know I had to go on that business trip today. It was for your sake as well as mine,' he said gently. 'God knows, I didn't want to leave you.'

'Just as you had to go on all those business trips when we were engaged, just as you hated leaving me then? she sneered, laughing angrily. 'You must think I'm really stupid!'

'Amanda, I——' He reached out to touch her shoulder and she flinched away from him.

'Don't touch me, don't ever touch me again!' She moved blindly through the room and into her bedroom to resume her packing. She had to get out of here. She couldn't take any more.

'Amanda, look, we've got to——' Drew stopped in her doorway in stunned amazement as he saw her suitcase. Then his eyes moved to the piles of clothes, the empty wardrobe, before coming to rest on her slender frame as she continued to pack, her back towards him. 'What the hell are you doing?' he demanded, the concern in his voice changing to anger.

'I'm leaving, what does it look like?' She was pleased there was no throb of pain or passion in her cool voice. 'I'm sorry to leave before the fashion show, but I'm sure you'll manage perfectly without me.'

'Like hell I will!' He moved and grabbed the clothes from her hand. 'You're not going anywhere.' There was a grim determination in his voice.

'Yes, I am.' She tried to pull the clothes back from him, all the time avoiding his eyes. 'You can sue me for breach of contract, if you want, but I'm going.'

'Why?' He bit the word out through clenched teeth. 'This morning you were clinging to me, needing me. Now suddenly you're leaving. Don't you think you owe me some explanation?'

'I don't owe you anything.' She stared at his chest, concentrating on his tie. 'This morning I wasn't thinking clearly—and last night was a mistake.'

'A mistake?' his voice rasped angrily. 'Look at me, Amanda, look at me and tell me that,' he demanded; there was a fury in his voice that made her tremble, but she ignored him and quickly turned to fasten her case. 'Look at me and tell me the truth,' he blazed.

'That is the truth,' she said calmly.

'God damn you!' He gripped her forcibly by the shoulders and turned her. 'Tell me why you're running away?'

She fought desperately to avoid looking into his eyes, but he wound his right hand up through her hair and tugged her head back so that she was compelled to face him.

'I'm not running away from anything.' She could feel hysterical sobs rising inside her. His face was a dark mask of fury close to hers, so close she could have reached up and kissed the tense line of his lips. She closed her eyes, willing herself to stay calm. 'I have to go, Drew,' she whispered unsteadily. 'You'll find another designer to replace me.'

'No, I won't. I'm not letting you walk out of my life again. I need you.' His voice was rough with emotion and her eyes flickered open wide, disbelieving.

'That's better, you shouldn't hide from me,' he murmured. 'You've got beautiful eyes, as wide and as deep as the sea and with as many moods.' He looked searchingly down into their green, shimmering depths. 'Sometimes they're wild and angry, stormy. Then they're calm, inviting, seductive.' His lips brushed a heated trail over her forehead and down to gently kiss her eyelids as they closed. 'You wouldn't believe the things your eyes told me last night,' he whispered.

Amanda struggled to maintain control of sanity as his lips moved to capture hers in a hard, hungry kiss, which threatened to explode into mindless passion. Even as her body clamoured for him, her mind was telling her something else. This man didn't love her. The words spun around her brain, giving her the strength to pull away from him.

'What's the matter, did the sexy Miss Lee turn you down tonight?' she demanded, her breath catching unevenly. 'Do you want me to stand in for her?'

'What?' His dark brows came together.

'You heard me,' she said harshly, trying to escape from his arms. His hold on her tightened painfully.

'I heard, but I didn't understand.'

She laughed and it was a bitter sound, devoid of humour. 'Drew, I know all about your affair with Jordan. I've known about it all along.'

'You think I'm having an affair with Jordan?' Drew sounded incredulous; if she hadn't known the truth she could have sworn his blank expression held innocence.

'I don't just think,' she said in a shaky voice. 'I know you've been having an affair with her since our engagement.'

He let go of her so abruptly that she stumbled back from him.

'Is that why you turned to James?' The question held explosive force, his face was dark with fury, his eyes suddenly murderous, holding hers, refusing to let her look away. 'Is that why you flung yourself into that idiot's arms?'

She could feel a deep heat seeping into her face. 'That's right, turn on James, blame everything on him!' Her eyes flashed fire at him. 'But let me tell you this: James never laid a finger on me, he was a gentleman. He was a true friend when—when you were—were cheating on me.' Her voice was starting to break with emotion.

'That night when I caught you with him?' He took a step nearer and she backed nervously away.

'I was upset.' She swallowed convulsively. 'I needed someone to talk to after I discovered you and Jordan...'

Drew's hand shot out to curl around her throat. 'And what about me?' he muttered. 'What about discussing it with me? My God, your opinion of me must have been rock-bottom! You couldn't even be bothered to accuse me to my face; instead you crept around secretly accusing me.' His hand tightened and she flinched.

'It wasn't any secret, Drew.' She put up a hand to try and break his hold. 'In fact, I think I was the last one to know about Jordan. Although it should have been obvious someone was getting your attention, and it certainly wasn't me.'

Drew released her and stepped back, staring at her as if he didn't know her. 'So you know I was having an affair with Jordan,' he said coolly. 'Where's your proof?'

Pain shot through Amanda at the casual way he was talking. 'I don't think there's much point raking over all this now. After all, it's dead and buried in the past.'

'You were judge and jury in the past.' Drew gave her an icy smile. 'You found me guilty and sentenced me without a trial. Now I want to hear the evidence.' He sounded as if he was controlling his anger with great difficulty. Amanda felt nervous as she looked up at him, and she shifted uneasily.

'Well?' He blazed the word and she jumped.

'You're frightening me, Drew—stop it,' she said, shrinking back.

'Frightened? You deserve to be damn well terrified.' Drew's jaw hardened. 'Now, tell me what this so-called evidence you have is.'

'You were seen going abroad with her,' Amanda told him through clenched teeth.

He made an impatient motion with his head. 'Yes? What of it? I've never made any secret of the fact that I employ the woman.'

'But do you really have to take her with you wherever you go?' Amanda drawled sarcastically. 'You brought her here to Paris when we were engaged; everyone knew about it, everyone was talking about it.'

'And who is this mystical everyone?' he persisted.

'Well—well, Kezia Van Slyke was telling everyone at——'

'Van Slyke—my God, that obnoxious, prattling old busybody!' Now he really looked as if he was going to explode. 'I don't believe anyone would be stupid enough to listen to her.'

'Are you calling me stupid?' Amanda glared at him.

'Yes, I damn well am!' Drew glared right back. 'Who else is on this lynching mob?'

'You think this is all very amusing, don't you, Drew?' she said stiffly. 'But I know it's all true because I happened to have caught Jordan at your hotel suite in London.'

'Jordan works for me,' he reminded her bitingly.

'Do you take all your female employees to bed? Is that what last night was all about?' she flung at him.

'Last night was about two people who care about each other,' Drew said quietly. 'You found Jordan at the London hotel suite because I reserve it for staff. I have done so ever since our engagement. If you remember, I spent my time in London at your house in those days, and no——' he went on firmly as she was about to interrupt, 'no, I have never slept there with Jordan; I've never slept with the woman, full stop. Our relationship is strictly business; we've had a few working lunches, but our conversation never goes beyond tax returns and assessment figures. If you think that's romantic, then——'

'You're lying,' Amanda interjected swiftly. 'How can you lie to me like that?' Her face was hot with rage, her voice held a bitter sting. She had hidden her jealousy for so long that now it was escaping she couldn't control it. 'Jordan told me, she told me all about your affair the day I caught her in your hotel room, and now you're engaged.'

Drew's face darkened. 'I don't know what the hell you're talking about.'

'There's no point denying it, Drew. I know it's the truth.' Her eyes suddenly filled with shimmering tears. 'Anyway, what's the point in arguing like this? The fact still remains that you're going to marry that woman.'

For a moment there was deathly silence, then suddenly he started to laugh.

'Don't you take anything seriously?' She swung viciously to face him. 'How dare you laugh about something so—so——' Her voice broke and she was horrified to feel bitter tears streaming down her face.

'Oh, Amanda!' Suddenly she was in his arms, all traces of amusement gone as he held her close. 'Where on earth did you get the absurd notion that I was going to marry Jordan?'

'You announced it at my father's party in London. Everyone heard you!'

'Announced it?' For a moment he sounded completely nonplussed. 'Amanda, the only announcement I made at that party was about the new manager I had appointed for Hunter Fashions.'

'The new manager?' she echoed him, bewildered. 'But I thought—Jordan told me——' She came to a confused halt.

'What exactly has Jordan been telling you?' he demanded harshly.

'That you love her, that you're going to marry her.' She couldn't see his face properly, it was a blurred shadow of colours through the haze of her tears.

'She did what?' The sudden anger in his voice was volcanic. She could feel it tensing his every muscle. 'The woman must be crazy—there's never been anything between us. Amanda, you've got to believe me, that woman and I have never shared as much as an intimate smile.'

The urgency in his voice made her heart lurch with sudden hope. 'You don't love her?'

'Love her?' His voice wavered angrily. 'Amanda, at this precise moment I'd like to go down there and strangle that viper, and I just might do it if you don't tell me you believe me.' He pulled her close against his chest again. 'Darling, please tell me you do. I can prove it, we can go downstairs now and confront Jordan. But please, just have a little trust in me before we do. It's so important to have faith and trust to build a relationship on.'

She wiped the tears away from her pale skin and stared up at him; she could hardly dare believe what he was saying to her, and yet there was such deep sincerity in his voice, and something else, something that made her

breath catch in a sob. She knew suddenly that her accusations had hurt him deeply.

When she didn't answer him, his grip tightened on
her. 'All right, let's go and see Jordan,' he said grimly,
moving her towards the door.

'No!' She shook her head, her eyes filled once more
with tears. She knew now with absolute certainty that
there was no need to hear anything Jordan had to say.
Drew was telling her the truth. She could hear it in his
voice, see it in his face. She blinked her tears away and
looked at him through sea-green eyes. 'Drew, I'm sorry,'
she whispered. 'I shouldn't have accused you like that,
I should never have believed those things about you. I
should have trusted you when we were engaged. It was
just that I felt so alone. I know you have every right to
be angry with me, but please don't hate me. I—I couldn't
bear it.'

'Hate you?' He sounded incredulous. 'How could I
hate you when I love you with all my heart?'

She looked up in wonder and her heart seemed to stop
beating as he bent his head and kissed her lips hungrily.
'Don't leave, Amanda,' he said raggedly as she pulled
away from him. 'I don't want you to walk out of my
life again. The mess we've made of our relationship is
as much my fault as yours. I neglected you when we
were engaged. I was so tied up with work that I didn't
realise we were growing apart. Then I leapt to con-
clusions as well—God, I've never been more jealous of
anyone in my life than I was of James. When I thought
that you loved him—that you were going to marry
him——' His voice trailed off bitterly.

'I would never have married James,' she told him
quickly, unable to endure the look of torment on his
face.

'I don't think I would have allowed you to,' he said
grimly. 'My life was so empty without you. I kept in
constant touch with your father just to hear what you
were doing, and if you still had James in your life. When

he told me he was going to sell the business I leapt at the chance of getting close to you again.'

'You mean you did buy the business because of me?' Amanda's eyes were shining with wonderment.

He nodded his head. 'I'm afraid so—I knew it was the only chance I had to be near you. But even then I couldn't get James out of your hair. I couldn't fathom just exactly what stage your relationship with him was at. One moment I knew you weren't really in love with him—the next I was consumed with jealous rage.' He sighed. 'It wasn't until I held you close last night that I finally was sure, and then, when I arrived back and you were so cool——' His voice was raw with emotion.

'Oh, Drew, I love you so much,' she burst in. 'It was just that I thought you and Jordan——'

He crushed her towards him fiercely, and his lips smothered her next words. 'Tell me again,' he demanded as he lifted his head.

She smiled shyly. 'I love you, Drew, with all my heart. I always have, there's never been anyone else.'

He let his breath escape on a ragged sigh. 'From now on, my love, you're not going to go anywhere without me. There's no way I will ever be parted from you again.' Suddenly he was swinging her up into his arms and moving towards the bed. 'When I think of all the time we've wasted, the stupid misunderstandings that we allowed to creep between us because of my neglect.' He shook his head.

She placed a tender finger over his lips. 'The fault wasn't just with you,' she whispered. 'If I hadn't been so insecure, things would never have got so out of control.'

He swept the suitcases off her bed and laid her down tenderly. 'We've both made a lot of mistakes, my darling, but I intend to rectify them all.' He looked at her delicate oval face and the heavy fall of her red-gold hair. 'I want to share all my life with you, Amanda; will you marry me?'

Her emerald eyes were filled with love as she whispered, 'Yes,' and kissed his lips gently.

'I suppose we'll have to wait until after the fashion show,' she said some time later as she cuddled into his arms.

'The way I feel now, the fashion show can wait.' His powerful arms brought her even closer. 'You are the most important thing in the world to me.'

She kissed the side of his face and then his throat with teasing lips. 'That doesn't sound like the businessman I know and love.'

He grinned. 'From now on, sweetheart, you're top priority. I'm not about to go through the torture of anything coming between us again. Come to think of it, first thing tomorrow that Jordan woman is going.'

'It doesn't matter now, Drew,' she said dreamily, so much in love that she could actually feel sympathy for the woman. 'I suppose I can't really blame her for loving you.'

'Well, I can, and she's going,' Drew said firmly, then he looked down at her and smiled. 'And it won't be to Bermuda. I think Iceland is more suitable for her.'

Amanda laughed, winding her arms around his neck, secure and happy in his love. 'Come to think of it, we could fit in a quiet wedding ceremony before the show. I have a wonderful design for a dress all lined up.'

Harlequin Presents

Coming Next Month

Available in September wherever paperback books are sold, or through Harlequin Reader Service:

In the U.S.
901 Fuhrmann Blvd.
P.O. Box 1397
Buffalo, N.Y. 14240-1397

In Canada
P.O. Box 603
Fort Erie, Ontario
L2A 5X3

**From America's favorite author
coming in September**

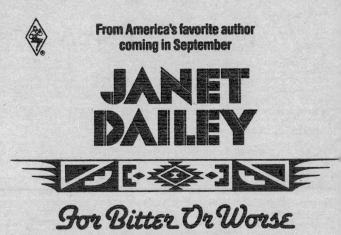

JANET DAILEY

For Bitter Or Worse
Out of print since 1979!

Reaching Cord seemed impossible. Bitter, still confined to a wheel-chair a year after the crash, he lashed out at everyone. Especially his wife.

"It would have been better if I hadn't been pulled from the plane wreck," he told her, and nothing Stacey did seemed to help.

Then Paula Hanson, a confident physiotherapist, arrived. She taunted Cord into helping himself, restoring his interest in living. Could she also make him and Stacey rediscover their early love?

Don't miss this collector's edition—last in a special three-book collection from Janet Dailey.

If you missed *No Quarter Asked* (April) or *Fiesta San Antonio* (July) and want to order either of them, send your name, address and zip or postal code along with a check or money order for $3.25 per book plus 75¢ postage, payable to Harlequin Reader Service, to:

In the U.S.:	In Canada:
901 Fuhrmannn Blvd.	P.O. Box 609
Box 135	Fort Erie, Ontario
Buffalo, NY 14269	L2A 5X3

Please specify book title with your order

JDS-1

HARLEQUIN'S WISHBOOK
SWEEPSTAKES RULES & REGULATIONS
NO PURCHASE NECESSARY TO ENTER OR RECEIVE A PRIZE

1. To enter and join the Reader Service, affix the Four Free Books and Free Gifts sticker along with both of your other Sweepstakes stickers to the Sweepstakes Entry Form. If you do not wish to take advantage of our Reader Service, but wish to enter the Sweepstakes only, do not affix the Four Free Books and Free Gifts sticker to the Sweepstakes Entry Form. Incomplete and/or inaccurate entries are ineligible for that section or sections of prizes. Not responsible for mutilated or unreadable entries or inadvertent printing errors. Mechanically reproduced entries are null and void.

2. Whether you take advantage of this offer or not, your Sweepstakes numbers will be compared against a list of winning numbers generated at random by the computer. In the event that all prizes are not claimed by March 31, 1992, a random drawing will be held from all qualified entries received from March 30, 1990 to March 31, 1992, to award all unclaimed prizes. All cash prizes (Grand to Sixth), will be mailed to the winners and are payable by check in U.S. funds. Seventh prize to be shipped to winners via third-class mail. These prizes are in addition to any free, surprise or mystery gifts that might be offered. Versions of this sweepstakes with different prizes of approximate equal value may appear in other mailings or at retail outlets by Torstar Corp. and its affiliates.

3. The following prizes are awarded in this sweepstakes: ★ Grand Prize (1) $1,000,000; First Prize (1) $25,000; Second Prize (1) $10,000; Third Prize (5) $5,000; Fourth Prize (10) $1,000; Fifth Prize (100) $250; Sixth Prize (2500) $10; ★ ★ Seventh Prize (6000) $12.95 ARV.

   ★ This Sweepstakes contains a Grand Prize offering of $1,000,000 annuity. Winner will receive $33,333.33 a year for 30 years without interest totalling $1,000,000.

   ★ ★ Seventh Prize: A fully illustrated hardcover book published by Torstar Corp. Approximate value of the book is $12.95.

   Entrants may cancel the Reader Service at any time without cost or obligation to buy (see details in center insert card).

4. This promotion is being conducted under the supervision of Marden-Kane, Inc., an independent judging organization. By entering this Sweepstakes, each entrant accepts and agrees to be bound by these rules and the decisions of the judges, which shall be final and binding. Odds of winning in the random drawing are dependent upon the total number of entries received. Taxes, if any, are the sole responsibility of the winners. Prizes are nontransferable. All entries must be received by no later than 12:00 NOON, on March 31, 1992. The drawing for all unclaimed sweepstakes prizes will take place May 30, 1992, at 12:00 NOON, at the offices of Marden-Kane, Inc., Lake Success, New York.

5. This offer is open to residents of the U.S., the United Kingdom, France and Canada, 18 years or older except employees and their immediate family members of Torstar Corp., its affiliates, subsidiaries, Marden-Kane, Inc., and all other agencies and persons connected with conducting this Sweepstakes. All Federal, State and local laws apply. Void wherever prohibited or restricted by law. Any litigation respecting the conduct and awarding of a prize in this publicity contest may be submitted to the Régie des loteries et courses du Québec.

6. Winners will be notified by mail and may be required to execute an affidavit of eligibility and release which must be returned within 14 days after notification or an alternative winner will be selected. Canadian winners will be required to correctly answer an arithmetical skill-testing question administered by mail which must be returned within a limited time. Winners consent to the use of their names, photographs and/or likenesses for advertising and publicity in conjunction with this and similar promotions without additional compensation.

7. For a list of our major winners, send a stamped, self-addressed envelope to: WINNERS LIST c/o MARDEN-KANE, INC., P.O. BOX 701, SAYREVILLE, NJ 08871. Winners Lists will be fulfilled after the May 30, 1992 drawing date.

If Sweepstakes entry form is missing, please print your name and address on a 3" ×5" piece of plain paper and send to:

In the U.S.
Harlequin's WISHBOOK Sweepstakes
P.O. Box 1867
Buffalo, NY 14269-1867

In Canada
Harlequin's WISHBOOK Sweepstakes
P.O. Box 609
Fort Erie, Ontario
L2A 5X3

Offer limited to one per household.

© 1990 Harlequin Enterprises Limited   Printed in the U.S.A.

LTY-H890

COMING SOON...

For years Harlequin and Silhouette novels have been taking readers places—but only in their imaginations.

This fall look for PASSPORT TO ROMANCE, a promotion that could take you around the corner or around the world!

Watch for it in September!

★

PASS